Songs of Summer

a Novel

By

Lara Gardner

Published by Hemingway Publishers
Cover design by Hemingway Publishers
ISBN: Printed in the United States

Visit My Website: https://authorlaragardner.com/

Table Of Contents

Chapter 1 2007..1

Chapter 2 1996..15

Chapter 3 2007..25

Chapter 4 1996..37

Chapter 5 2007..47

Chapter 6 1996..61

Chapter 7 2007..63

Chapter 8 2022..79

Chapter 9 2007..87

Chapter 10 2022...103

Chapter 1

2007

Charlotte

Charlotte Masters grabbed a bottle of chilled Moscato from the fridge and a stemless, polka-dot wine glass from the cabinet and took them to cozy in on the couch of her newly redecorated family room. Thanks to inspirations and coupons from Hobby Lobby, her condo was getting a little makeover. She lit her favorite Yankee Candle on the coffee table and was immediately comforted by the scent of Cranberry Chutney. Charlotte poured her first glass of wine and decided to watch reruns of *Golden Girls* while she thought about the conversation with her dad earlier that evening. He'd always made jokes about how he couldn't wait for the day she'd move back to Eagle Valley, often making light of it with a grin. But today, there was a distinct shift in his tone, a deeper, more genuine longing lacing his words. Today, it almost sounded like he was pleading with her to come home; he actually sounded quite sad. She thought again about going for a visit, but between finishing her dissertation and going on job interviews, she hadn't made the time. She would go soon, she promised herself. It had been almost two years since she was able to make it home. It had been two years since her mother died.

After the funeral, Charlotte thought she should drop out of college and move back to Eagle Valley to help with the family's farm. She knew deep down, though, that her mom would want her to finish her graduate degree. She always made sure Charlotte knew how important education was, so Charlotte went back to her condo in Durham, NC, and threw herself into school. Every chance she had, she asked her dad about hiring someone to help with the farm, but he reassured her that everything was under control. She thought about calling the Preston boys to see if they might be able to pitch in until they could find someone to help full-time, so she made a note in her Things-To-Do notebook. She had no idea that her dad had already found some help. Charlotte watched one more episode, put her wine glass in the overflowing kitchen sink, and tossed the bottle in the trash. Deciding to wash the dishes, she turned her thoughts to the interview she had tomorrow morning.

The next morning, after she put the finishing touches on her makeup and extra hairspray on her long, wavy curls, Charlotte looked in the mirror one more time. She was impressed with how put together and professional she looked this morning. There were no outward signs of the entire bottle of wine she drank last night or the crippling loneliness she felt deep in her soul. Today's interview was with Dr. Elizabeth Marsh, a pediatric psychiatrist in the suburbs just outside Raleigh, NC. Dr. Marsh runs her own small family practice and is looking to add a pediatric therapist. Although she is just offering part time, Dr. Marsh's office would be a great place to start her career.

Charlotte was attracted to this job because of the small practice size and its convenient location. It was just a three-mile drive from her condo. The drive would be a breeze in her sporty white convertible Cabriolet. Her Aunt Lindsey and Uncle Brian gave it to her for graduation in 2003, and she loved it. When she climbed in the car, Charlotte wasn't quite sure if she was feeling more nervous than excited or vice versa. She checked the rearview mirror and headed off to meet Dr. Elizabeth Marsh.

Later, as she sat in the car with the engine off, reflecting on the interview, Charlotte felt a sense of pride. She was proud of herself professionally, and Dr. Marsh seemed impressed by her. She knew her mom would be proud of her, too. Tossing her hair up in a messy bun, she grabbed her sunglasses, put the top down, and decided to go for a drive to clear her head. Despite the interview going well, a knot lingered in her stomach, and she wasn't sure why. Though Dr. Marsh was very nice and seemed happy with all her answers, Charlotte couldn't quite tell what she was thinking. Dr. Marsh told Charlotte what an accomplishment it was for her to be graduating early from Duke University with a Master's degree in Clinical Child and Adolescent Psychology. However, Charlotte felt like Dr. Marsh seemed more interested in what her future plans were rather than what she would be bringing to this office. She came across almost as if she was surprised Charlotte wanted to work in a small practice. She questioned her a lot about her interest in trauma cases and inquired about her five and ten-year plans. She even asked about her willingness to relocate. That one surprised Charlotte the most.

As if on autopilot, Charlotte drove through Starbucks and ordered her usual venti, vanilla, sweet cream Cold Brew with extra cream. She sat in the typically long drive-thru line and texted her very best friend, Paul. They had been inseparable since Kindergarten, and even though it had been awhile since they actually talked, it never seemed to matter. They would pick up right where they left off, just like they always did. She sent him a short text to ask what he was up to and wondered what he'd have to say about her having an interview there, back home, in Eagle Valley. Then she called her classmate, Kelly, to cancel their lunch plans because she was going to enjoy the scenic route home. The winding roads through the rolling Appalachian Mountains soothed Charlotte's soul. She felt herself disconnecting from her thoughts and concerns and instead let her thoughts stay with Paul. *How had so much time gone by since they last talked?* She was disappointed when she didn't hear back from him right away but sighed at the thought he was busy.

Later at home, Charlotte threw on her favorite pair of gray yoga pants, some comfy socks, and an old oversized Hurley sweatshirt. She smiled when she realized it was Paul's sweatshirt she'd borrowed and apparently adopted back in high school. Grabbing her laptop off the table, she settled in to learn more about Dr. Elizabeth Marsh's life.

Elizabeth

After a long day of seeing patients and three great interviews, Dr. Elizabeth Marsh was exhausted. She put her feet up on the desk to think about her day. She felt good about her patients' progress and made a note to send a referral to South Hampton Speech Therapy. Elizabeth then settled in to review the interviewees. The first was a graduate student from Duke. She had all the right credentials - and then some. The second interview was with a teacher-turned-therapist whose enthusiasm to help every single child with every single one of their problems was undeniable. The third interview was with a retired military veteran with a new life outlook. He said that helping young children overseas who were struggling with PTSD made him realize he could help other small children handle their big emotions. He told Dr. Marsh he moved to Raleigh for a fresh start after finishing school, and Elizabeth knew that feeling all too well. The decision was easy, so she picked up the phone. The call after that, however, would be the one to change someone's life.

After hanging up with Scott, the veteran who enthusiastically accepted her job offer, Elizabeth dialed her ex-husband, Atticus. They had been divorced for over a decade, yet their bond had only deepened with time. Despite the split, the wounds that had once torn them apart seemed to have healed, and their relationship was stronger now than ever before. Elizabeth had moved to the Raleigh-Durham area shortly after the divorce to start her own practice, determined to carve out a new life for herself. And even after all these years, Atticus still believed in her dreams. He went to Eagle Valley to be Chief of Pediatrics at Blue Ridge Memorial Hospital.

"Hey!" Elizabeth said when Atticus answered the phone, "How was your day?"

"Elizabeth! I'm glad you called! I was just thinking about you. You wouldn't believe what happened today," he paused, "but you called me! What's up?" He loved hearing her voice.

"I interviewed a woman today; she's finishing her master's in clinical child and adolescent psychology from Duke. I absolutely loved her, Atticus, but she needs to be up there with you. She's a perfect fit for the hospital. She wants to work trauma, and has completed extensive internship work with some extreme cases. She's an incredibly impressive and promising young woman. Atticus, she wouldn't be using her full potential working for me," Elizabeth went on, "so what would you think about calling her?"

Atticus quickly responded, "Do you think she'd relocate?"

"Well, you won't believe this, but she's from Eagle Valley. Her family is still there. I asked her a lot of questions about her long-term plans and goals. I think she'd seriously consider relocating. Atticus make her a generous offer. Make sure she knows she'd be the Chief of Pediatric Psychology, running her own brand new, state-of-the-art trauma unit!"

"I will, I will! Text me her information," he said. "I will call her now. And Elizabeth," he paused. "Thank you."

"Of course! You know I'm so proud of you!"

"You're too good to me," he said in a cheeky voice.

Elizabeth smiled and he could almost hear it through the phone. "I wouldn't have it any other way. Now, tell me about your day."

"That can wait 'til later," he said. "I want to call her right now. I'll call you back, okay?"

"Can't wait!" she exclaimed.

Elizabeth loved talking to Atticus; his voice was both strong and soothing, and it had made her happy for a very long time. Today was no different, she thought, as she closed her office for the night.

Charlotte

When the phone rang, it startled Charlotte. She thought it might be Paul since she still hadn't heard back from him, but she didn't recognize the number. However, she recognized the Eagle Valley area code and answered.

"Hello?" Charlotte asked.

"May I speak to Miss Charlotte Masters, please?" a strong male voice asked.

"This is she," Charlotte answered quickly.

"Miss Masters, my name is Dr. Atticus Richards. I am the Chief of Pediatrics at Blue Ridge Memorial Hospital in Roanoke, Virginia. I'm calling with a job opportunity; might you have a minute to talk?" he asked.

Charlotte paused but replied, "Of course, Dr. Richards. I'm sorry; where did you say you're from?"

The corners of his lips curved, and he explained, "I am the Chief of Pediatrics at Blue Ridge Memorial Hospital in Eagle Valley, Virginia. I got a call from Dr. Marsh down there in Durham; she said she interviewed you this morning."

Her eyes brightened, and she leaned in, her hands unconsciously fidgeting with the edge of her notebook. "Oh! Yes, I did! She did!" Her voice rose with a hint of disbelief as she looked up, her smile fading into a thoughtful frown. "But I don't understand what my interview with her has to do with your hospital in Roanoke."

"I have just expanded our Pediatric Department to have its own Psychology Department. This includes both in and out-patient services. I am looking for a Chief of Pediatric Psychology. You come highly recommended by Dr. Marsh, and I would be honored to meet you. The facility is brand new and in its final construction stages. It has been added to the back of the hospital. I am in the beginning stages of putting together a top-notch team, but I need a Chief, and I want someone who really understands the needs of kids who have experienced trauma, too. Dr. Marsh and I think you'd be the perfect fit! Can I convince you to come to Eagle Valley and meet me in person?" Atticus finished and held his breath in anticipation.

Stuttering her words at first, Charlotte exclaimed, "W-wow! I am truly flattered, and I don't even know what to say! Other than yes! I would be honored! Thank you!" Her eyes lit up, and a huge smile came over her face.

Charlotte and Atticus talked for another fifteen minutes about the program and job details. They agreed she would arrive at the hospital next Monday, and there would be three days for tours, interviews, meetings, and social events.

Charlotte thought about calling Dr. Marsh and thanking her for the referral, but that would have to wait until tomorrow morning, she thought to herself, realizing the time. Instead, it was the perfect time to call Kelly. An interview for a Chief position called for some cocktails, girl talk, and shopping! With butterflies in her stomach, she grabbed her purse and ran out to meet Kelly at the mall. Besides, Paul never did text her back.

Paul

Paul Stone settled into his usual spot at the counter in Molly's Diner, the worn stool creaking under his weight. He ordered his usual breakfast. It wasn't the only place to get hot coffee and a homemade breakfast, but it was absolutely his favorite. As he wrapped his hands around the steaming cup, he sighed. A second cup of coffee was a must to recover from that night shift. His partner, Justin, and he had been tracking reports of someone lingering in the woods behind the Preston Ranch again. They spent last night's shift combing the thick, dark woods and found some empty beer cans, food trash of no significance, and a few raccoon traps, but that was it. *There was nothing unusual about that*, he thought. Paul wondered why anyone would be back in those woods in the first place or how an outsider would even find that part of the woods. They would cover more ground on their shift tonight but at the moment, he was exhausted and ready for some sleep today.

His thoughts were interrupted when the phone rang. Before he could even say hello, Charlotte was excitedly yelling in his ear. Paul smiled and walked outside of the diner. He listened as she told him all about yesterday's interview with Dr. Marsh and the phone call from Dr. Richards. She told him she would be coming to Eagle Valley this weekend and he should cancel his plans. Then she started yelling at him for never returning her text last night. Paul heard her pause for a second.

"Wait, what are you up to? Are you busy?" She said, sounding out of breath. He smiled and actually heard himself laugh out loud. It was the first time in a long time that he had heard himself laugh.

"Of course, I'm busy, but that never stops you!" he teased. He didn't realize how much he actually missed the sound of her voice. Besides, he would stop the world if it meant talking to Charlotte.

Molly Stone noticed his smile when he walked outside on the phone as she ran an order to another booth by the window. She hadn't seen her son smile like that in a very long time, so she knew exactly who was on the other end of that phone. *Those two have always had something special*, she thought to herself, but she wasn't sure if either of them truly knew it. Molly was cashing out a lady at the counter when Paul returned to the diner.

"Was that Charlotte?" Molly asked.

"Yes, she's coming to Eagle Valley this weekend. She's got an interview at the Blue Ridge Memorial Hospital for Chief of Pediatric Psychology. She was talking so fast I could barely keep up with the details. I never knew she was considering moving back home. She never said anything about it."

"That's wonderful, good for her!" Molly said.

Paul furrowed his brows, his gaze shifting. He was puzzled. "Did you know anything about it?" he asked.

"No, nothing at all," Molly said, trying to contain her over-the-top excitement.

"I wonder what changed her mind!" he said to his mom.

"Some things just have a way of working themselves out." She gave him a wink, patted the counter, and turned to walk away.

On his way home from the diner, Paul heard a song on the radio that took him back to a certain memory from a long time ago. He wasn't sure if it was the song on the radio or hearing Charlotte's voice that made that one summer night come back to life for him. Actually, he did know. It was Charlotte. He drove with the windows down, letting fresh air and sunshine into the truck. He tried to think about the busy week ahead, between working night shifts and trying to finish up the project at his side job. He thought staying busy would be a perfect distraction for him because if he thought about her much more, his heart would explode out of his chest. Paul knew

11

that would happen the moment his eyes would land on her this weekend anyway.

Paul lived in one of those old brick ranch houses on the outskirts of Eagle Valley. Since he loved having projects to do, he had worked through updating the inside for the past several years. Coming into the house today, he was suddenly aware of how messy it was. He told himself he'd clean up before the weekend, but it had to wait for now. Paul knew he needed to sleep since he had to return to work at eight o'clock tonight, so he went into his bedroom. That's the thing about working night shifts, he thought, you just leave the shades drawn and lights off so that whenever you get the chance to sleep, you can just crash. He put his gun and badge on top of the dresser, unbuttoned his uniform shirt, and tossed it onto the floor, not before realizing he couldn't keep his thoughts away from Charlotte. Having her home for a week would be perfect. Everyone felt the huge hole she left after her mom's funeral, but she left an even bigger one in Paul's heart. He tossed his undershirt on the floor, unbuckled his belt, and sat on his bed. He started to text her but couldn't think of anything worthy to say. He took off the rest of his clothes and slid into bed.

Paul woke up in time for a workout before dinner and a shower. He recently converted the garage into a gym, installing sleek custom floors, a new elliptical, a full-weight set, and surround sound speakers. He even added a sauna in the corner. He was proud of himself for the way he finished off the room and that he splurged on all the new equipment. Paul was good and sweaty by the time he was done. He grabbed a sweat towel and sat on the weight bench. He reached for his phone and texted Charlotte.

"Hey!" he wrote. He liked the suspense of what she'd say back.

"Hey yourself!" She wrote back with a winking emoji. "What's up?

"I just wanted to say hey. I didn't exactly get many words in earlier!" he poked. "I just finished working out. My shift starts at eight."

"Nice. Listen," she typed to him, "I know we really haven't talked lately, and I wanted to say I'm sorry." She pushed send.

"No worries, we've both been busy with life. It's all good. So, anything in particular you want to do this weekend?" he asked.

"Not really, but I'm sure we'll figure something out. So, what's new at work? Anything exciting with the cops in Eagle Valley?"

"Of course!" he was going to embellish this one big time. "Last week was a high-speed chase after the bank robbery, and just last night, we found a body in the woods!"

"WHAT?" She typed in all caps.

"Yeah, I can't believe you didn't see it on TV. It was all over the news! Oh wait, they don't show the news on the Golden Girls channel, do they?"

"Wait, what? Oh, shut UP!" She wrote back, laughingly. "See, you just secretly love Golden Girls, too!"

"Well, of course, you know it's my favorite!" He smiled and wrote.

Charlotte finally said, "Go catch the bad guys! Love ya!"

"Love ya, bye," he said, as naturally as they had been saying it to each other for the past twenty years.

Chapter 2
1996

Charlotte

So, do you love her?" Charlotte asked with a subtle worry in her voice.

"I don't know," Paul quickly replied. "How do I know if I'm in love? We're only 15. What kind of question is that?"

Charlotte tilted her head slightly, her eyes searching mine with a teasing glint, "Okay, but you love me, right?" she asked, drawing out the word "me" as her lips curled into a playful pout.

Looking over at her, he smiled, "Always."

"Is she coming to the party next weekend?" Charlotte hoped for a different answer than the one she knew she'd get.

"Of course she is," Paul replied with a hint of frustration in his voice, his brow furrowing as Charlotte tried to hide the slight roll of her eyes. "Why?"

"Ug, because it's THE annual party! And, I mean, she doesn't go to school with us, won't know anyone, and never wants to hang out with us anyway. You never talk about her, and she has a bad reputation. I just don't get what you like about her!" Charlotte was getting all worked up and frustrated because she just wanted to shout out loud that there would never be anyone good enough for Paul. No one could ever know or see him the way she does.

Paul nearly laughed out loud, but the frustration in his tone lingered. "What's the matter with you? Why are you freaking out? You don't even know her, and you don't like her. Plus, we all hung out all day, and now it's just us! Stop freaking out!" His words came out fast, but the edge of confusion softened his voice. The air between them thickened their emotions, a tangled mess of unspoken words and unresolved tension.

It was as if they stunned each other and it was suddenly silent. They lay down on the cool concrete by the pool, shoulders just barely touching, the night pressing in around them. The stillness of the moment felt surreal as they stared up at the August sky, the stars shimmering above them like quiet witnesses to everything they couldn't say.

Charlotte thought about how fun the day had been - like most other Saturdays, playing outside, listening to music, swimming, working on the boys' trucks. A day with Paul, Kyle, and Luke was always perfect.

Paul reached over and held Charlotte's hand. He squeezed it, and Charlotte squeezed it back.

He looked over at her and said, "You know you'll always be my best girl, right?"

"I know," she said as she exhaled the breath she didn't know she was holding. She held on tight because she didn't want that moment to end. The radio was playing in the background, and when Don't Stop Believin' came on, they laughed. It was their song. They were always laughing about where they would go if they took a midnight train to anywhere.

Charlotte sang, "Some'll win, some will lose."

Paul jumped to his feet and belted, "Some are born to sing the blues!"

And in perfect unison, they finished the stanza, "Whoa, the movie never ends; it goes on and on and on and on."

The sun had started to go down, and it was Charlotte's favorite time of day. The rays of the sun kissed the leaves on the trees, creating a magical oasis around them. Paul tore off his shirt, running to the diving board, setting up for the perfect cannonball. He leaped into the air, muscles taut and glistening under the pool lights, but Charlotte didn't notice his tanned body and sculpted abs. He aimed his splash to soak Charlotte and nailed it perfectly. She screamed in surprise, but before she could make a run for it, Paul was out of the pool in a flash. In one swift motion, he scooped Charlotte over his shoulder, her laughter mingling with his, as they plunged back into the water together. They surfaced, laughing hysterically, they could barely catch their breath - it was one of those moments they'd always remember.

Just then, Paul's mom came out with chips and Cokes and made herself comfortable on a lounge chair by the pool. She asked about their day and enjoyed listening to what Charlotte thought must be the same stories over and over again. Molly genuinely cared about what they did and who they were with. She never seemed to get bored with the teenage stories. Charlotte loved talking to Molly.

"You two have been best friends since forever, ya know," she said with a giggle and grin.

"We know, Mom, you tell us all the time," Paul called out from the diving board.

"Well, it's important to have a person who makes you laugh and always has your back. You're just teenagers, and you've already found that person. It's someone that knows your story and walks through it with you," she shared with her sweet, southern voice. She continued to talk, but Paul had already tuned her out as he set up for a backflip. Charlotte listened, treasuring Molly's words, "Never take this friendship for granted." Molly winked at Charlotte.

Calling out from the diving board, Paul said, "Yeah, well, just in case either of you needed a reminder, I'm the best friend anyone could ever have!"

Charlotte smiled and looked at Molly. "If he only knew!" She said.

Hours had passed, so it was pitch black when Paul and Charlotte walked down the dirt path to Charlotte's house. They were walking in silence when they heard something rustling in the bushes. Charlotte jumped and ran off because she thought something was coming to get her. Paul jumped, too, and chased after her. By the time he caught up to her, they were both laughing so hard they could barely breathe.

"You're such a scaredy cat!" Paul yelled.

"Oh, because you're so tough? Good luck walking back home without me," she said sarcastically.

"Do you think I need you with me all the time?" he teased.

"I'm pretty sure we both know the answer to that!" The laughter continued the rest of the walk home. It was the perfect end to another perfect day.

The lights were out at Charlotte's house, and they both knew what that meant. She could go to her room and hopefully get some sleep without anyone knowing. Her mom was sick, and she didn't want to make any noise to bother anyone.

Charlotte hugged Paul and said, "Thanks for walking me home."

"You know you don't have to thank me, Char," he said sincerely.

"I know but I say it anyway! Love ya!" She said with a wink as she turned and walked away.

Paul heard her lock the door and then looked at her window, waiting. The light turned on, and she stood there giving him that smile that always lit up the night. She blew him a kiss, and he walked away, knowing she was safe.

Becky

Watching Paul and Charlotte from the woods was something Becky had become comfortable doing. A few months ago, she found a cove-like spot where three trees wove together. It was tucked away enough that no one would ever find her, but she had a great view of Paul's backyard and part of his house. Becky started coming here after she met Paul last spring. They didn't go to school together, so she had to find things out for herself. She justified her continued voyeurism by convincing herself it would make her a more supportive girlfriend since she would know what he liked to do, what made him laugh, and who his friends were.

Tonight, she watched Paul and Charlotte walk down a dirt path away from the backyard, now knowing he was walking her home. Becky had watched the two of them hang out and swim for hours. It's like they were inseparable, and Becky didn't like it. *Shaking the cluster of overgrown holly bushes to scare them was hilarious,* she thought to herself. Charlotte screamed, but soon they were both laughing uncontrollably, tangled in each other's arms. Their laughter was so intense they could hardly stand. As they caught their breath, She couldn't help but feel a little confused—she didn't understand this girl, Charlotte.

20

She and Paul were always together, but they weren't dating. They did everything together but never actually did anything fun. Becky thought that the more she watched them, the more she'd understand, though she was still waiting for that to happen. Her thoughts were interrupted when she heard Paul coming back up the path. She stood up, brushed off her jean shorts, and walked to the path. She casually strolled towards him so he wouldn't realize where she had been. Upon seeing her, Paul was surprised, to say the least. She couldn't tell if he was happy to see her, but she wouldn't let that stop her.

"Hey!" Becky squealed. "Whatcha up to?"

Paul was surprised, confused, and a little pissed off. "Becky! What are you doing here? It's so late. Did my parents tell you where I was? How did you know I was back here?"

"I was driving home from my friend's house and decided to see if you were up. I parked down the street so I wouldn't wake up your parents," she said, shifting on her feet, her fingers nervously fiddling with the edge of her hoodie. Her eyes darted around before landing on his, a small smile twitching at the corners of her lips. "I was looking to see if your bedroom light was on or if you were in the backyard, and I heard you coming up the path! Want to hang out?" She laughed a little too quickly, tucking a stray strand of hair behind her ear.

"Um, it's a little late. A bunch of us hung out today, and I'm pretty tired."

21

"Not too tired to walk Charlotte home, though, right?" she asked sharply. "I mean, I assume that's where this path leads? How will we ever get any time alone at night if you're always tired or always with Charlotte?"

"Wow. I don't really know what to say. I'm sorry? Yeah, I'm sorry. Maybe we can sit out here for..." Paul couldn't finish his sentence before he felt her tongue in his mouth. She practically launched herself at him, her hands gripping the back of his neck with an almost desperate urgency. Her tongue slipped past his lips, hungry and demanding. Paul kissed her back instinctively, but there was something frantic in the way she moved.

They were pressed up against the old oak tree, her body flush against him, the rough bark digging into his back as she pushed her breasts against his chest. It was too much, too fast. The heat of her touch burned through his skin, and for a moment, his breath hitched – he wanted this, didn't he? But something inside him snapped, a knot tightening in his stomach. He broke away, stepping back and wiping his mouth, feeling the tension ripple between them.

"What the hell?" she yelled, pushing him away. Her face was flushed with anger, "Don't you want to be with me?"

"I've got to go. I'll talk to you tomorrow," he said quickly, without meeting her gaze. "Sorry."

"Well, this is going to be a lot harder than I thought," she whispered to herself as she watched Paul go into the house. When Becky was sure he was inside, she disappeared back into the woods.

Paul

Paul lay in bed and thought about how weird it was that Becky just showed up on the path tonight. He didn't even really know that she knew about the path. He wasn't sure how she knew that Charlotte was over or that the path led straight to her house. But Becky was hot, like super hot, and she was interested in him. He knew her reputation, one that often made adults raise their eyebrows and everyone whisper in the hallways. She was rebellious and made daring life choices. Paul was exactly the opposite. So before he fell asleep, Paul thought about whether he wanted to pursue a relationship with Becky.

Chapter 3

2007

Charlotte

A s Charlotte drove into Eagle Valley, a wave of nostalgia washed over her, making her heart swell with a mix of joy and bittersweet memories. The familiar winding roads, now lined with taller trees, seemed to welcome her home with open arms. Riding with the windows down, the crisp air carried the scent of pine and freshly cut grass, a comforting reminder of her childhood. The sun's rays filtered through the dense canopy, casting dappled light across the road like a warm embrace from the past. Every turn revealed a piece of her history—the old church where she spent countless Sundays, the schoolyard where she and Paul had shared their first secrets, and the little bookstore where she discovered her love for reading. But it wasn't just the memories that moved her; it was the subtle changes, too. The once quiet Main Street now buzzed with new life, with fresh paint on the storefronts and a new coffee shop where the old hardware store used to be. Yet, despite these changes, the essence of Eagle Valley remained the same—a place where time seemed to slow down, where the worries of the world melted away.

She was so excited about this week of interviews, activities, and visits with family and friends. It was just what she needed. If she took this job, and it's quite the dream job, she would be happy, fulfilled, and close to everyone she cared about. She took a deep breath, turned right onto Main Street, and pulled up to Molly's Diner.

She loved the familiarity of the diner. Everything down to the black and white floor tiles, smells of coffee, and homemade bread were as delightful as always. Charlotte noticed that the Saturday lunch bustle was beginning to ramp up so she decided to take a seat at the counter, the same spot she and Hannah used to always sit for chicken sandwiches, peanut butter milkshakes, and girl talk. Suddenly, Charlotte heard a familiar voice bursting through the kitchen doors. Molly's excitement could be heard a mile away. She hurried to Charlotte and hugged her tightly. Charlotte hugged her back. Neither of them knew who needed that the most. Charlotte sat back down at the counter, and before she knew it, she had a large iced coffee and her surrogate mom all to herself.

"Tell me everything. Paul tells me nothing!" Molly said with a big smile. "How are you? How is school? How's the love life?"

"Well, did he tell you I was coming into town for an interview at the hospital?" Charlotte asked, already knowing the answer.

Without missing a beat, Molly said, "He did! But you have to tell me all the details. And tell me your plans while you're here. Does your dad know you're in town? Have you seen Paul yet? Oh, this is so exciting, it hasn't been the same without you around here the past few years." Molly's energy was contagious!

Taking a long sip of her iced drink, she savored the flavor before answering Molly. "I did talk to my dad," she started to share, "I talked with him for a while last weekend and then for a few minutes this week. I told him I was coming into town. Have you seen him lately? He didn't sound quite right on the phone, and it's been bugging me. I can't put my finger on it."

"I know your dad is having some issues at the farm, but he's made it clear to everyone that he's just fine. I take over meals whenever I can, and Paul has been spending time over there when he can, too. Oh, Charlotte, he is going to be so happy to see you," Molly said genuinely, wishing Charlotte already knew about the problems her dad was dealing with. Instead, she changed the subject. "Where are you staying while you're here?"

"Oh! I'll be at the Bed and Breakfast! I can't wait to see what Shirley has done with the old Brookhaven Estate. Have you been inside yet?"

"Oh yes! They had a little opening ceremony, it's so nice! The rooms are so cozy, and she's decorated each one differently, but all with the same cozy feel. I'd spend a night there any time!" Molly leaned in, her eyes sparkling with curiosity. She wanted to know everything - the ins and outs of the job, how the interview went, every little detail. But a quick glance at her watch sent a wave of guilt through her. "So, what's next? What are you up to today?"

"I think I'll go settle in at the B and B and then head over to see Dad," Charlotte said. She didn't realize how heavy her words sounded. "Paul and I have plans to meet later because he said he was working a side job today."

"Well, I hope you have a wonderful day, sweetie. Glad you're home!"

She finished her coffee, waved to Molly, and walked out to the warm mountain air. Charlotte sat in her car, a heaviness settling over her chest. It suddenly dawned on her that by leaving right after the funeral—because she thought it was best for her—she hadn't considered how it might affect the people in her life. Did they need this reconnection as much as she did?

With her arm out the window and wind blowing through her hair, a song came on the radio that took her back to a certain memory from a summer night a very long time ago. Charlotte smiled and decided she'd go see her dad first.

Paul

Paul had been going to Bud's farm a few days a week for about the last year. Obviously, he needed the help, and Paul secretly needed the company. Paul also knew Bud was too proud to ever ask for help, let alone hire some help. When it began, about once a week, Paul would just go over and ask what Bud was up to that day, offering his company. Sometimes, they would just talk, and sometimes, Bud would let him cut the grass or fix the tractor. Other days, he helped with handyman work around the house. Not only did he enjoy the hard work and extra money, but it also helped Paul feel closer to Charlotte. He thought Bud felt the same way. A few months later Bud offered Paul the job of designing and building a small cottage on the back of the property by the pond. After all this time working together, a friendship had grown between the two men. They had an unspoken understanding and believed that Charlotte would come home if they built this cottage.

Today, they were working on the railing along the cottage's front porch. Paul needed the work at the ranch today because it would make the day go by faster. He didn't have to work again until Monday night, but he was going to see Charlotte tonight. He was so excited about seeing her that he wasn't even sure how he'd be able to wait until tonight.

They thought they heard a car on the gravel drive, so they got on the ATV and made their way up to the house. A familiar white convertible was parked, and their hearts leaped out of their chest. Charlotte stepped out into the sunlight with a breezy dress and a bright smile. Her long brown hair was piled on top of her head and perfectly windblown from the drive.

"Dad!" she exclaimed, her voice catching as she practically threw herself into his arms. He lifted her slightly off the ground, their embrace so tight it felt like they were trying to make up for lost time. Tears welled up in her eyes as they clung to each other, unwilling to let go. When Bud finally released her, she wiped her eyes quickly and turned to Paul, her heart still pounding from the overwhelming wave of emotion.

"What are you doing here?" she said as Paul scooped her up, twirled her around, hugging her. She felt an intensity in his arms, an intensity she never noticed before. "I thought we were meeting up later tonight!"

Paul looked over at Bud and then back at her, smiling. "We are! I just came by to help your dad with something, but we're all finished up. I'm actually on my way out," he explained. "Bud, I'll see ya. Charlotte, call me when you're headed back to town." Paul couldn't stop smiling as he walked to his truck. His heart was full again.

Charlotte

The visit with her dad was enjoyable and easy; they talked for over an hour. He listened intently to all the details of the Chief job position, and she listened to all the projects he had going on around the farm. The project on the farm he didn't mention, though, was the cottage. Not yet. It was a wonderful conversation, and they each felt reconnected.

Before she left, she hugged her dad and said, "What can I do for you, Dad? What can I help you with?" she asked genuinely.

Hugging her hard, he said, "You're here now, buttercup. That's all I need."

Bud walked her to the car and hugged her again. "I'm glad you're here, Charlotte. I'm so proud of you. I can't wait to hear how things go on Monday. I'm here if you need me," he said. Charlotte couldn't remember the last time she heard those words from him. It was just what she needed. What she didn't know, though, was how much he needed it, too.

About twenty minutes later, Charlotte arrived at Brookhaven Bed and Breakfast, her heart fluttering with anticipation. As she parked, she took in the sight before her. The place was nothing short of breathtaking, a perfect blend of history and charm. Shirley had clearly worked hard to restore the old estate. The brick was original, with dated grout and everything. Charlotte stepped out of the car, her eyes tracing the elegant lines of the house. All the windows, framed by pristine white shutters, glistened in the soft afternoon sunlight. The front doors were grand, painted a deep, welcoming shade of red, and the entryways beckoned her inside as if promising comfort within. The landscaping boasted large azalea bushes and magnolia trees, and a smoothed cobblestone pathway led from the long driveway to the front of the house. She noticed another pathway she could tell went around to the back where the horses used to be. She couldn't wait to see if Shirley still kept horses back there. Charlotte opened the heavy wooden front doors and rang the bell on the little desk in the entry room. She could feel herself relax from the sound of the crackling fire. Just a few minutes later, Shirley came out from behind the desk.

"Well, Miss Charlotte Masters, as I live and breathe. I can't believe it! Look at you! If it's possible, you're even more gorgeous than the last time I saw you," Shirley said with effervescent joy. "Let's get you all settled into your room. I saved a very special one for you!"

Shirley had been a friend of Charlotte's mom, Samantha, for as long as she could remember. As young girls, Shirley and Samantha always dreamed of opening a bed and breakfast together one day. The girls had made plans, had ideas for locations and buildings, and had particular thoughts for decor and layout. When Samantha was diagnosed with stage four astrocytoma, just eight months before she died, the girls made a withdrawal from their joint dream fund and bought the old Brookhaven Estate. The house had been vacant for just a short time and was the perfect place for Shirley to carry on the girls' childhood dreams.

Shirley showed Charlotte to her room and said, "If you need anything, I'll be in the kitchen. Make yourself at home, sweetie!"

With a thanks and a smile, Charlotte closed the door, set down her bags, and sighed. She felt the weight of her world just lift from her shoulders. She smiled as she looked around the room. Shirley was right; this room was special. Charlotte didn't know yet just how special it actually was. The B and B had been renovated with all modern amenities, but it still had the Eagle Valley charm. The scent of warm vanilla sugar welcomed her inside. The queen-sized bed was covered with a raspberry and white duvet and massive amounts of oversized pillows. Charlotte thought for a minute about how she could just melt away if she just crawled in for a nap. Tempting. An oversized chair took up the far corner next to an antique dresser. The bay window had been turned into a cozy reading nook with even more oversized pillows. Charlotte also noticed a blanket and a book thoughtfully placed on the bench.

She unpacked her clothes into the dresser and sat at the antique vanity. She was organizing the contents of her cosmetic bag when the phone rang. *It was Paul.*

Answering with an excitement she tried to contain, she casually said, "Hey, what's up?"

"How did it go at your dad's?" he asked.

"Well, umm, I don't really know how to describe it. It was pretty great! We had an easy conversation, and it was actually really comfortable. He didn't make me feel bad about being gone for so long. I thought he was mad at me, but when I was leaving, he said the craziest thing. When I asked him if he needed anything, he said that having me here was all he needed for now. Like wow, I didn't see that coming," she continued, "The last few times we'd talked on the phone, he's seemed…umm…different…distracted maybe? I really thought it was all because he wanted me to be at home and not back at school after Mom died. So, I thought our visit would be awkward, with weird expectations, but it really wasn't. I think we both feel better now that we've seen each other in person. But I don't know, maybe I really should have stayed here after Mom died. I really love it here."

Listening with care, Paul thought again about how he's always been her person and wouldn't have it any other way. "That's awesome! I'm glad you had a nice visit. I know he's missed you."

"Sorry, I didn't mean to ramble on, but thanks for saying that," she said, collecting herself. "So, what's up? What are you up to? Did you figure something out for tonight?"

"It's fine. I was just calling to see how your visit went and what you think of the B and B! I overheard my mom saying something about amazing views of the new barn and horses. Have you seen it yet?"

"No! I haven't even had a chance to look out there!" Walking over to the bay window, Charlotte pulled the soft lace curtains back and had to catch her breath when she saw Paul. It was Paul with his truck and a handful of wildflowers she knew he had just picked from the side of the house because the dirt was falling from the roots. It was Paul outside her window, just like the old days. She laughed and said, "Wait. What? Paul, what the hell are you doing here? You're ridiculous!"

"Well, I just thought I'd swing by to see those horses I hadn't seen yet. Then I thought we could just meet up here since I'm already here?" He said, laughing. "Just come on, we've got celebrating to do!"

"You're crazy! I need to freshen up. I'll be down in 10 minutes."

"Take all the time you need; I'll wait out front. We're meeting everyone at Black Ox," he said as he climbed back in the truck. "Drinks and dancing!"

Before hanging up, she squealed, "Paul. Thanks for this!" He could feel her excitement and sincerity through the phone.

Ten minutes later, Charlotte blew through the front door of the B and B and straight into Paul's old pickup. It was like time had never passed. They talked the whole way to Blue Ox, and it was as easy as breathing.

Chapter 4
1996

Paul

I t was the day of the party, and Paul wanted to mow the lawn while it was still cool in the morning. He pulled the lawn mower out from the old, rickety shed on the side of the house and pushed it to the front yard. The early morning sunlight kissed the dew drops on the grass, creating a shimmering blanket. He wasn't quite sure why he noticed it this morning, but he laughed, knowing that Charlotte would love it. *She sees beauty in everything and romanticizes seemingly trivial details of the world around her.* He thought about tonight's party and how awesome it was going to be. It wasn't just a small group of his best friends hanging out; this was a bring your friend and their friend kind of party. He knew how lucky he was that his parents were happy to host the annual end-of-summer bash. They were amazing parents. He thought about how much he loved that everyone always wanted to hang out at his house except Becky. She never wanted to come to his house or spend time with his family and friends. So, when she said she'd come to the party, Paul was thrilled. She had promised this time, and he hoped his friends would finally see how fun and cool she was. More than anything, though, he really wanted Charlotte to like her.

His thoughts were interrupted when his brother, Mike, came screeching in the driveway like a race car driver. It was only nine in the morning, Paul thought; where had he been? He knew not to ask because the answer would be something mean or degrading, and he didn't feel like getting into a fight. Besides, he had other things to think about than what his delinquent older brother was doing.

As Mike walked from his car to the house, he yelled, 'Hey loser, you missed a spot."

Paul felt his blood start to boil, and he couldn't help himself, "Drop dead," he yelled back. He hated his older brother.

Charlotte

Hannah came over so they could get ready for the party together. Charlotte was already distracted because Paul's girlfriend was going to be at the party. She had met her a few times, but they had never spent any real time together. Her name was Becky and Charlotte didn't like her from the second she met her. She was always hanging all over Paul and not interested in anyone else. Charlotte knew what Becky wanted from him, and she'd be glad to be the one to tell her that she was not going to get it.

"This is going to be awesome," Hannah squealed, running up the steps. "Let's wear tube tops and jeans!"

"My mom would die, you know that."

"That's why I brought sweaters, too. We wear these until we get out of the house," Hannah explained.

"You think of everything," Charlotte said with a smile.

"This is why you love me," Hannah gave her friend a wink and cheesy smile.

The girls put on their favorite mixed tape and laid all their makeup on the counter. It was a dazzling array of every color, shade, and hue a teenage girl could ever dream of wearing. They worked methodically at shaping their brows and carefully applying foundation, then blush.

"Not too much, just enough," Hannah said. The girls worked on their makeup together like musicians in an orchestra.

"I think Chris is going to try to kiss me tonight," Hannah squealed.

Silence.

"Charlotte?"

Nothing.

"CHARLOTTE!"

"Yes! Right! Wear that color!" Charlotte quickly said.

Without missing a beat, Hannah continued with full excitement and anticipation, "Aren't you listening to me? Oh, I bet he's an amazing kisser. I mean, I know I've never kissed anyone else, but I just know he's going to be a great kisser. I wonder where we're going to kiss. Do you think he'll do it in front of other people? Maybe it will be outside, like under the stars! That would be so romantic! Don't you think so? What do you think?"

No response.

"CHARLOTTE!" Hannah smiled at her friend. "What is going on with you? You're not even paying attention to me!"

"I'm sorry, I am. I hear you, I promise. It IS so exciting, and I am so excited for you. I'm just distracted. Paul said Becky is going to be there tonight. There's something about her I don't like." Charlotte looked at Hannah apologetically as she realized she was sucking all the fun and energy right out of the room. She felt bad for that, but she couldn't completely get it out of her mind.

"Whatever. We don't even know her, and you never like any girl he likes. Who cares anyway? We're going to have fun, and that's all that matters! Where's the curling iron?" Hannah tried to keep the excitement going. She refused to let some other insignificant girls ruin their fun!

Charlotte pulled the curling iron out from under the sink and handed it to her friend.

"She's going to break his heart," Charlotte said as she caked on her mascara.

"Charlotte! We're 15! He doesn't love her; he doesn't know what love is! And news flash, you can't save him from a broken heart," Hannah said flippantly. "He'll be fine, and you need to get over this. Besides, isn't LUKE coming to the party?"

"Yes!" Charlotte yelled, almost instantly snapping out of her sorrowful daze.

Just then, Spice Up Your Life started playing. The girls cranked it up and danced like they didn't have a care in the world.

Paul

The living room was filling up with friends and friends of those friends. Everyone was laughing and dancing together. Paul floated the room, took care of the music, and talked with everyone around the house. A sea of awkward teenagers in uncomfortable clothes danced so close to each other that Paul couldn't tell whose sweat was whose. He wanted to dance with Becky right now. He scanned the room again but didn't see her yet. He also hadn't seen Charlotte, which was weird, because she and Hannah were usually the ones to get the party started. Paul joined Luke and Chris by the door, trying not to look like they were waiting for something - or someone.

"Great turnout!" Luke said.

Paul still couldn't believe Becky wasn't there, and neither was Charlotte. This is not how this party was supposed to be. And then, like gusts of wind from an east coast hurricane, Charlotte and Hannah blew through the back door and into the life of the party.

You could feel the music through the walls. House of Pain's *Jump Around* had everyone on the dance floor. Hannah grabbed

Charlotte by the arm and pushed through the crowd, shouting *Hey* to all their friends. They eventually made their way to where Luke, Kyle, and Paul were standing.

"Hey guys," Hannah yelled with excitement. "This is awesome!"

Paul walked over to Charlotte, his shoulders slumped and a blank expression masking his emotions. She felt the pit in her stomach tighten. She already knew.

"Hey, what's up?" she said, avoiding what she knew he was going to say. "Let's go dance!" she suggested, her voice unnaturally bright as she tugged lightly on his arm.

Paul hesitated, exhaling softly. "She's not here," he said quietly, his gaze dropping to the floor as the weight of his disappointment settled between them.

"She'll be here, don't worry," she said, pretending to care.

Charlotte

She didn't want to talk about Becky, so Charlotte pulled Paul to the dance floor with all their friends. They quickly fell into a rhythm of dancing together. It felt natural, easy, and fun. They fit together perfectly, no matter what kind of music was playing. The girls were singing, holding their hands up in the air, and jumping to the beat. The boys, as usual, rolled their eyes at the girls but still joined in the fun.

The night seemed to fly by, so many friends, so many songs, so much laughter. Charlotte caught a glimpse of Chris leading Hannah out the front door so she went out back for some welcomed rest and fresh air. She sat on a chair by the pool and wondered where Luke had gone. She lost track about an hour ago. *Whatever.*

"Boo!" Paul yelled, grabbing the chair she was sitting on.

"AHHH! What the hell?" Charlotte screamed and jumped out of the chair. She punched him in the gut.

"She never came," he said as they sat down with their feet in the pool. "I can't believe she didn't come at all."

"That sucks, I'm sorry."

"No, you're not. You're glad she wasn't here," Paul snapped.

"I am not," Charlotte snapped back.

"Yeah, right. You didn't want her to be here anyway. You barely know her, and you hate her," he said, not really knowing he was picking a fight.

"First of all, I don't even know her, so how can I hate her? I hate the way she acts and how she never does what she says she's going to do. But you think that I'm glad to see you upset? What the hell is that?" Paul just stared at her. "Don't take your shit out on me just because you're mad at her for not coming."

"Okay, okay, I'm sorry. I didn't mean it. I just don't get why she didn't show up." Then they sat in silence for what felt like forever - *a good forever.*

"Charlotte?" He asked quietly. "Promise me you'll always show up,"

Looking over at him, Charlotte whispered, "Always."

The silence lingered, but it was a comfortable one. The sounds of the party inside were starting to fade. Then, Hannah's scratchy, exhausted voice broke through, calling out to Charlotte.

"I've gotta go," she said. "Unless you want me to stay?"

"No, I'm good. See ya later!" Paul said, watching the two girls run off. As they walked away from the pool and disappeared down the path to Charlotte's house, Paul smiled when he heard Hannah yell, "Best! First! Kiss! Ever!"

"Tell me everything," Charlotte enthusiastically said to her best friend, looping their arms together.

While they walked, Hannah told Charlotte all about her first kiss. They talked all the way home, and then, as they were getting ready for bed, Charlotte thought about the sadness she saw in Paul's eyes when she left. She was sorry that Becky never showed up because she hated how sad it made him. What she didn't know, however, was that the real sadness she saw had nothing to do with Becky at all.

Becky

The night of the party, Becky met up with this guy she knew from work. They had been hooking up for a few months now. The commitment was casual, and the sex satisfied her needs. Instead of going to Paul's party, she wanted some fast, fun sex. When she was done, Becky got out of his car and walked back to her car, where it was parked at the diner. She wanted to see if Paul's party was as lame as she thought it would be, so she drove towards his house.

In the woods at her usual hiding spot, Becky could hear the party winding down. She watched Paul and Charlotte ending the night together by the pool. It seemed like that's how they ended every night. After a few minutes, she saw Charlotte and some other girl walk down the dirt path together. Paul stayed out there, watching the girls leave, and then sat for a while, just looking off into the distance. She considered going out to talk to him but didn't want to give up her secrets yet. Instead, Becky waited for Paul to go inside before returning to her car and driving away.

"I think I've been watching the wrong person," she thought.

Chapter 5

2007

Paul

When he woke up late Sunday morning, Paul got dressed to head over to Bud's farm. Though there wasn't much left to do on the cottage itself, he wanted to bring over the rocking chair and side table for the front porch. It hadn't taken him too long to make, but he was proud of his craftsmanship. He loaded up the truck and turned onto Slippery Rock Rd. The drive to the farm was about twenty minutes long, and his mind drifted to last night and how much fun everyone had. He laughed about the way he surprised Charlotte at the B and B and their effortless conversation in the truck. The Black Ox did not disappoint either. It was loud and crowded, and everyone wanted time with Charlotte. It felt like 1996 all over again with the dancing, the songs, the friends. Except this time, the party included tequila shots and axe throwing.

Paul glanced across the room at Charlotte, noticing the way her shoulders slumped, her fingers absently tracing the rim of her glass.

He let out a slow breath, realizing just how much he needed this night out - probably as much as she did. His fingers drummed lightly against his thigh, a tension in his chest easing as he took her in. She caught him looking, offering a tired smile that didn't quite reach her eyes. Paul returned it with a nod, feeling the weight of the day slip off his shoulders. This night was exactly what they both needed.

Paul drove down the dusty road leading to the cottage past the main entrance to the farm. When he arrived at the cottage, Molly was already there.

"Hey, Ma," Paul said, opening the door. "How's it going in here? It looks really good!"

"Thanks, kiddo! How was last night?"

"It was loud and crowded and lots of fun," Paul said. "I brought the rocker and table. Come see how it looks!"

In a tattered shirt and work jeans, Paul muscled the rocker over his head and carried it to the front porch. He put it down next to the large potted pansies, which he was sure was his mom's doing. He also made a small side table resembling a whiskey barrel that fit perfectly along the rocker's other side.

Just as Molly came out to see the porch, Paul's phone rang. He answered, listened, and quickly said, "Got it. I'm on my way."

"I've got to run, Ma. Sargent Miller said there are more reports of someone in the woods. I've got to pick up Justin and head out there. Tell Bud hi for me!"

"Be safe," Molly called out. She watched her son jump in his truck and drive back down the dirt road. She was so proud of the wonderful man he's become. Then her mind wandered to that early summer morning when she woke up because he was out there cutting the grass without even being asked. His father would be so proud of him, too. Turning to go back inside, she smiled at the rocking chair and table. It was perfect.

Charlotte

She thought about getting up and going for a walk, but the pounding headache kept her in bed. She wasn't sure if it was from the tequila shots, the loud music, or the bright morning rays of sunlight piercing through the edges of the curtains. Her mind told her it was a whole lot of all three. Last night was so much fun, she thought to herself. It was great to see Hannah and Luke, of course, but some other high school friends, Karrah, Amy, and Laura, were there, too. They all caught up on what's happening in their lives and how everyone's family is doing. *It's funny how people change over time*, she thought, and *funny how some people don't.*

Hannah and Luke had invited Charlotte to come to their house for the afternoon today. Hannah was the girl who married her high school sweetheart. She and Luke stayed in Eagle Valley, and both attended Radford University. Hannah is now a Kindergarten teacher, and Luke is a CPA. They were happy, and Charlotte loved spending time with them. Over the past two years, Hannah visited Charlotte in Durham when she could. She understood why Charlotte had a hard time visiting Eagle Valley after her mom died, so she made most of the trips. They always needed their girl time. Charlotte thought about canceling her plans with them this afternoon and just spending the day lounging here. But if she didn't go out to visit today, she wasn't sure when she'd have time once the interview days started. Charlotte thought about how much she really missed them. They weren't expecting her until later in the afternoon, which did give her plenty of time to be lazy and then get herself ready. She stayed in the most heavenly, cloud-like bed she's ever slept in and thought about Paul. Something seemed different with him last night. Not like something was wrong, she thought, but more like something was on his mind. Maybe it was work? She texted him, and he quickly wrote back that he was at a work emergency and would text her later. She felt relieved. It's got to be work.

Around ten o'clock, Charlotte climbed out of bed, put on the pink, plush robe from the bathroom door, and slipped her feet into the flip-flops. She walked down the hallway to the kitchen for a piping hot cup of coffee and maybe a quick chat with Shirley. Back in her room, she decided to snuggle up in the cozy reading nook. The oversized pillows were amazing, and she wasn't sure she'd ever seen so many on one bench before. Snuggling into the pillows and wrapping herself up in the yellow toile quilt, she took a long sip of coffee and realized the book in her hand was Louisa May Alcott's *Little Women*. It was Charlotte's favorite book and her mom's favorite, too, which made her get a little choked up.

Charlotte's fingers brushed over the deep creases in the spine of the book, feeling the history in its worn edges and the little tear that marred the book cover. She nestled into the corner of the couch, intending to lose herself in a chapter or two when something fluttered out from the middle pages - a thick, aged piece of stationery. Her heartbeat quickened as she reached for it. The paper felt heavy with significance, its edges slightly yellowed with time.

Unfolding it slowly, her breath caught when she recognized the handwriting—perfectly written cursive in blue ink. It was familiar, achingly so, tugging at memories she thought she had buried. The slant of the letters, the elegant loops—they were unmistakable. Her chest tightened as her eyes skimmed over the words. This wasn't just any note—it was personal. A whisper from the past she wasn't sure she was ready to face.

She swallowed hard, her heart pounding in her throat, and began to read.

My Darling Charlotte,

Remember how much we loved reading this book together? Reading with you was one of my favorite times of the day.

"Oh my God," Charlotte whispered.

If you're reading this note, it means you have reconnected with Shirley and Eagle Valley. That makes me so happy. Your roots are strong here, and you can always call it home. I asked Shirley to give this letter and my copy of this book to you when she thought the time was right. You have sacrificed a lot over the last eight months, sweet girl, and done it all with patience and grace. You are a treasure, Charlotte, don't ever forget that.

Charlotte couldn't believe what she was reading. She was holding her mother's book and a handwritten letter. She stared at the stationery. She remembered it from always being on mom's desk. It was an old secretary's desk passed down through her family, and mom kept it in the corner of the kitchen. We teased her about it being her 'command post' since it seemed like she ran the world from that desk. The heavy paper complimented the gold embossed monogramming of her mother's initials – SAM, Samantha Anne Masters. Charlotte put down her coffee, ran her finger over her mother's beautiful cursive writing, and continued reading.

One of the hardest truths in all of this is knowing I won't be a part of the beautiful love story that will unfold in your life. Your soul mate is out there. Enjoy the journey. Let yourself fall in love and let it feel right. You will be the most beautiful bride, Charlotte, and he will be the luckiest groom. Let Shirley and Molly fill in my shoes, okay? They will help you plan all the details and choose your perfect wedding dress. Let them shower you with all the love, laughter, and guidance. Hold on tight to Dad. Let him spoil you however he wants. You are the most important thing in his life.

Thank you for taking care of me. I wish I could have spared you from seeing me so sick, but I couldn't imagine going through this without you by my side. It is my hope that one day, you will share this book with your own daughter. Teach her about life and love and loss and the power to stay the course. Show her what true strength is. Let her make choices, make her own mistakes, and find her own path. And in the end, if she's even half the daughter you are to me, you will be the luckiest mom in the world, too. Being your mother has been the honor of a lifetime.

I am with you always,

Mom

Charlotte wasn't sure how long she'd been holding her breath, but when she let it out, she cried a big, hard, ugly, cleansing kind of cry. She stared at the letter for what felt like forever. She was in shock, she was taken back, she was sad. But also, in that moment, she was peaceful. Shirley was right; this was a special room - a room to remember Samantha. Everything about this room captured the essence of her, the class and calmness, the ability to make anyone feel comfortable. It was perfect. Charlotte could feel a piece of her heart healing. A piece she had been ignoring for the past two years. She opened the book to Chapter One, and she could feel her mom all around her while she read.

She got herself ready and drove out to see Hannah and Luke. They weren't going to believe this story at all!

Charlotte

Later Sunday night, Charlotte was snuggled in, drinking a glass of wine and reading more of *Little Women* when her phone started ringing. It was Paul. Before she could say anything, he was already talking to her.

"Hey!" He said loudly, sounding either out of breath or exhausted, or both. "Are you asleep?"

"Not anymore!" she teased. "Just kidding, no, I'm just reading. What's up?"

"Can you come over?" he said with a shaky voice.

Without hesitation, Charlotte said, "On my way." She grabbed her keys and ran out the door, still wearing her pajamas and the big, fluffy robe.

She turned into his driveway and threw her car in park. She wasn't sure what was going on or what she'd find when she got there, but Charlotte ran up the walkway and blew through the front door. Paul was sitting on the couch with a beer. The TV was on, and the lights were dim. He turned around when she came flying in.

"Paul? What's up? What's wrong?" She said, practically out of breath.

"Don't you knock?" he said without turning around.

"Nope," she said flippantly. "What is going on?"

"You're never going to believe this," he said as she threw her things on the coffee table and plopped down at the other end of the couch. He handed her a beer. She grabbed a blanket and took a long sip of the beer. She wasn't sure if she was ready to hear whatever he was about to say. "Justin and I arrested the guys who have been causing issues in the woods for a few months."

"Well, that's great! That's a good arrest, right?" Charlotte tilted her head, her lips curling into a sweet smile. She reached over and gently brushed his arm. "No wonder you look exhausted!"

He nodded, rubbing his hand over his face, trying to shake off the fatigue. "Yes, but here's more. We've been trying to catch whoever was causing trouble in the woods, mostly behind the Preston ranch," he went on, his voice a bit gruffer now, "and it turns out it was Jason and Jackson Preston."

Charlotte blinked, her eyebrows furrowing in confusion. She shifted her weight, one hand absentmindedly playing with the hem of her sleeve. "Wait, what? The Preston boys? Why would they be messing around and hiding out behind their own house?" Charlotte asked.

"I don't know, honestly," he said, looking at her. "Apparently, they've been on a crime spree for a few years, running from cops. And get this: while they were on the run, they killed four people."

"Seriously?" She just stared at him.

"Char, there's more." She didn't like the way his voice changed when he said that. "When they searched the truck, they found in the woods, there were tons of notes, pictures, and pages of sketches in several different notebooks. All of the detailed descriptions of their stalking, tracking, and ultimate plans to burn an entire property here in Eagle Valley," he watched her staring at him. "Charlotte, your dad has been having issues at the farm for a while."

She stared at him. "I don't understand. What are you saying exactly?"

"Charlotte," he said to her calmly, scooting closer to her.

"What is it? Just spit it out!" she yelled at him.

He continued talking calmly, "A few months ago, your dad found the tractor's tires slashed and the fuel tank punctured. There was diesel all over the floor of the shed. There was also an empty cigarette pack with a lighter inside on the floor of the barn. Your dad also saw some sort of light moving down the side of his property two nights in a row. Apparently, standing on the front porch with a shotgun was not enough to scare off whoever was out there. So, I've been going out there every once in a while. I've been helping him do things on the farm but also being a second set of eyes."

She sat frozen on the couch, her fingers gripping the fabric, eyes wide, hanging on every word. Her breath hitched, and her chest rose and fell in quick succession as Paul continued.

"Charlotte, the plans that were found in the truck were months' worth of your dad's comings and goings, and the plans were of the farm," Paul said.

Her eyes flared, and her face twisted in shock. "WHAT THE FUCK? Like, what the actual FUCK! What does this mean? What are we going to do? PAUL! Holy SHIT!" Her voice climbed in panic, her movements frantic as she paced toward the kitchen, arms flailing.

"The Sheriff is over talking to your dad right now. Do you want me to take you over there?" Paul asked.

Paul

"I don't even know what to say! I don't know what to do! This is absolute insanity," Charlotte yelled. "All this time the issues at the farm were because of the Preston boys? I thought Dad was overwhelmed with the workload or that he was mad at me and falling into a hole of depression. Why wouldn't he tell me that weird things were going on?" She paused for a few seconds, and then her words slowed down. "I. Um. So. Paul? The room is spinning. I...I....don't feel so good." He ran to her just in time to catch her as she passed out. They both collapsed into a heap on the kitchen floor.

Paul absolutely hated upsetting her, but he knew she would want to hear all this straight from him. He had seen her flip out before, but he had never seen her pass out. He looked at her, unable to move. After a few minutes, Charlotte came to and smiled at him when she opened her eyes.

"Well, that was quite dramatic, even for you," he laughed. "How do you feel?"

"My head hurts," she said, sitting up. "What are we going to do? Where is my dad?"

Paul helped her up and to the couch. He set her up with pillows and a blanket, and then he brought her some Advil and a cold washcloth for her head. She told him she just wanted to stay here since it was so late, and he agreed. Paul reminded her that the Sheriff would take care of Bud and the property, and she would be safe with him. He's always made sure she was safe, and he always would.

Paul sat at the other end of the couch and put her outstretched legs over his lap. He put his feet up on the footrest and reached for the remote. He scrolled through the TV guide, and they decided on *Good Will Hunting*. They both seemed to settle in and relax a little, and Paul could feel Charlotte's breathing settle.

Looking over at him, Charlotte said, "Hey," and his gaze met hers. "Thank you for telling me. Thank you for making sure I'm safe."

"Always," he said with a smile, snuggling a bit closer. "Besides, I should be thanking you."

"For what?" she asked, crinkling her eyebrows.

"For always showing up."

Halfway through the movie, Charlotte fell asleep. Exhausted from it all, Paul dozed off, too. When they woke up the next morning, they were in exactly the same place.

Molly

The usual breakfast crowd was keeping Molly busy on Monday morning. "Now for some breaking news," Molly heard from the old TV. The WSLS anchor announced, "The Roanoke City Police Department confirms that the multi-state manhunt for murder suspects Jason and Jackson Preston has finally ended." Molly quickly turned the volume up, and the entire diner's attention turned to the TV. "The brothers were arrested yesterday in a densely wooded area of Eagle Valley. They have been charged with multiple counts of criminal mischief, criminal trespassing, stalking, and 4 counts of murder. Authorities say they are proud of the tireless hours, collaboration, and hard work of all law enforcement agencies involved." After the report, they showed the picture of the two police officers who made the arrest. Justin Whitlock and Paul Stone. Molly's mouth dropped open. She tried to call Paul, but there was no answer.

Molly called Charlotte to see if she knew anything about all this. She didn't know what time her interview was today, but she tried anyway.

"Charlotte!" Molly shouted when she answered the phone. "Did you hear about the Preston boys getting arrested? Have you talked to Paul? Apparently, he and Justin are the ones who found them in the woods yesterday!"

"I just heard it on the radio while I was driving to the hospital. My interview is in thirty minutes. I talked to Paul late last night. He was exhausted," she said vaguely. "I'm sure you'll hear from him today."

"I hope so! Let me know how your interview goes, okay? And Charlotte, you're going to be great!" Molly said, having no idea how much Charlotte needed to hear that.

"Thanks, Molly. Talk to you soon!" Charlotte hung up the phone and was proud of herself for not going into all the details of last night. She told Molly only what Molly needed to know and she needed to focus on her interview. The thoughts of the sweet tenderness of last night would have to wait until later.

Chapter 6
1996

Becky

Sunday morning, Becky sat next to her aunt in church. She thought attending every week would be a good way to mask her reputation. Becoming Paul Stone's girlfriend would help that, too, but it was going to be hard work. He was nice and honest and very straight-laced. She, on the other hand, was not the girl next door. She decided that Paul would be more like a project boyfriend than a long-term relationship boyfriend because she was going to have to put so much time and effort into getting what she wanted. It seemed like all he ever wanted to do was hang out at home, and Charlotte was always around. Becky realized she needed to get him away from his house to have some time alone with him. If she could sleep with Paul Stone, it would change everything.

To tune out the pastor's monologue today, Becky thought about that one Sunday back in September, the first time she saw Paul. She and her friends had been sunbathing on the rock bed and decided to go skinny dipping to cool off. She noticed him fishing down the river. One of the girls knew who he was, and Becky didn't hesitate to initiate a conversation when they just happened to drift nearby. They weren't shy about showing off their bodies, their breasts, and their carefree attitude. It wasn't until a little later that Becky noticed his parents and a girl she assumed was his sister were also there. Now, however, she knows Paul doesn't have a sister, and that girl with them was Charlotte. She decided right then and there to get Paul all to herself. His smooth, tanned skin, rock-solid physique, and brown tousled hair aroused her immediately. She'd have to get Charlotte out of the picture. Becky was going to make her lifestyle attractive to him, and that's exactly how it all began.

When church ended, Becky got up and walked with her aunt. She smiled at all the right people and nodded her head to all the comments about what a blessing she was to her aunt.

Paul

Paul decided he was going to skip family lunch after church, a tradition they've always had. His parents questioned him, but Paul just left. He didn't have a plan, but he was going to be with Becky. *Alone.*

Chapter 7

2007

Atticus

D r. Atticus Richards moved to Eagle Valley in 2000 when Blue Ridge Memorial Hospital opened its pediatric unit. Prior to that, he had a private pediatrics office in Richmond, VA. He and his wife of twenty years didn't agree on moving to Roanoke, so they amicably divorced, said goodbye, and moved away from Richmond. Atticus settled in Roanoke, accepting the Chief of Pediatrics position at Blue Ridge Memorial. Elizabeth moved to Durham, NC, and started her own practice. Despite moving to different cities and states, they remained incredibly close, as if the physical distance was merely a formality. Their bond endured, seemingly untouched by the divorce, which felt more like a logistical detail than a true separation. They continued to share their lives and support each other, proving that their connection was deeper than mere proximity. Atticus was happy as the Chief of a huge hospital. He loved that Elizabeth followed her passion for private practice. He felt strongly about supporting her no matter what. However, he hated divorcing her.

Atticus was prepared to greet Miss Charlotte Masters this morning at 9 am. He came to the hospital early to ensure he had everything in place for her time here. He stood in his office gazing through the expansive picture windows at the Roanoke River, its gentle flow a constant source of solace. The view was one of the many reasons he cherished this place. From almost every corner of the hospital, the river's presence was a calming influence, its shimmering surface reflecting the sky's ever-changing hues. The peaceful ripples offered a serene escape that brought a sense of tranquility to both patients and staff alike. He often found himself lost in a mesmerizing dance of light on the water, finding comfort in its steadfast serenity amid the hospital's demand.

Back at his desk, Atticus reviewed the itinerary he and his secretary had worked out. He wanted to make sure that Charlotte had plenty of time to do and see everything she needed to. He had planned for her to have time to sit and talk with all the right people. He wanted her to meet the other doctors, nurses, and therapists he had lined up. He planned a dinner out, too. But as far as he was concerned, between her resume and Elizabeth's recommendation, she'd be hired on the spot. He was thankful that Elizabeth thought of him and sent Charlotte on this journey. He was thankful for Elizabeth in general. His thoughts were interrupted when his office phone rang.

"Hello, Dr. Atticus Richards," he said inquisitively.

"So, are you ready?" the voice on the other end asked. It made Atticus smile.

"Hey, Elizabeth," he said. "I am ready! I'm looking forward to meeting her. I think I have all the plans in place, no thanks to Alice. I had to basically help her with all the planning. Remind me why I hired her," he went on.

"Alice is an experienced office coordinator and she thinks the world of you. She might not be the most self-driven or independent secretary by definition, but she's dependable and predictable," she explained. "It will be fine. Besides, you've got more important things to focus on right now. I can't wait to hear how it goes with Charlotte. Will you call me later?" she asked.

"No one else I'd rather call!" he said sweetly. Hanging up the phone feeling happy and confident, Atticus took a deep breath, adjusted his lucky necktie, and walked down the main lobby stairs to meet Charlotte.

Charlotte

The sun was shining as Charlotte stood on the sidewalk in front of Blue Ridge Memorial Hospital. The building was massive yet somehow inviting. It was five stories of mirrored glass, the kind that's hypnotizing with its reflections. She hadn't been inside since her mom's final days here two years ago. This hospital was where one chapter of her life ended, but standing here now, Charlotte could feel the start of a new chapter in her life. As she walked closer to the building, she was overwhelmed by the symbolic reflection. There she stood, with her notebook and new little red flats, against a backdrop of endless possibilities. Charlotte took a deep breath and walked inside to meet Dr. Atticus Richards.

The lobby of the hospital was as grand and beautiful as Charlotte remembered. It was filled with natural light and boasted a large staircase, a waiting area, and a 40-foot-long, curved welcome desk. Everyone at the desk had a smile on their face. Looking around, Charlotte noticed a man of great stature wearing a dark gray suit, which she figured was Dr. Richards. She smiled and approached him. Shaking his hand, Charlotte and Atticus exchanged pleasantries and he invited her for a tour of the hospital. They walked across the massive lobby, past the front desk, and started down the halls. Everything, she noticed, was so clean and orderly. Despite the hospital's 25-year age, it felt as though it had just opened its doors. The usual signs of wear and tear—peeling wallpaper, water-marked ceiling panels—were conspicuously absent. Freshly painted walls gleamed under bright lights, and the floors sparkled as if they had been polished just moments before.

She was given a quick tour of the departments, operating rooms, cafeteria, doctors' lounges, on-call rooms, supply rooms, and patient suites. Their conversation was easy and light. Charlotte found herself really enjoying his company, and Atticus knew she'd be the perfect addition to the hospital.

After the general tour of the hospital, Dr. Richards brought Charlotte to the pediatric building. The rooms and hallways were both calm and inviting. The artist put much detail on the seascape murals with soothing beach tones of whites, blues, and greens. It was tempting to run your hand down the wall, hoping to catch even a small feeling of being by the sea.

Dr. Richards introduced Charlotte to all the nurses and supporting staff around the area. Charlotte felt genuinely welcomed and at ease. Miss Catherine Moore, RN, was no different. She was in her office, and Dr. Richards led Charlotte in for introductions. Catherine was enthusiastic and warmly greeted them both. Charlotte guessed she was in her mid-to late-thirties; she wore trendy eyeglasses and the most fun, teal, donut-patterned scrubs. Dr. Richards explained that Catherine had been the head nurse of the pediatric unit for about eight years. Dr. Richards asked Catherine if this would be a good time for her to join us for the tour of the new psychology unit.

"Absolutely," she said. Catherine led them out a back entrance and down another sidewalk to a free-standing, newly built two-story building. The architecture mirrored the main hospital. Charlotte hadn't quite put together where they were going. "Charlotte, it's so nice to meet you in person finally! I've heard so much about you professionally, but I also can't wait to get to know you personally!"

"Thanks, that's so nice of you to say, and me, too," Charlotte replied warmly.

"Doc here," she said, tilting her head toward Atticus with a playful grin, "tells me you're originally from Eagle Valley and studied at UNC! You and I are scheduled to have coffee tomorrow

67

morning to go through the nuts and bolts of the preliminary plan for the psychology department," she went on, her hands making enthusiastic gestures as she spoke. "But I think we'll have lots more to talk about, too!"

"I can't wait!" Charlotte exclaimed, her smile widening as she clapped her hands together in excitement. Catherine motioned them to continue walking.

Dr. Richards and Catherine walked and talked to Charlotte, covering every inch of the building. This would be Charlotte's building. This brand-new, state-of-the-art building would be designed, stocked, and staffed however she wanted.

Back at the main hospital, they settled into Dr. Richard's office, where he went through an overview of the pediatric department. His position as Chief of Pediatrics was to oversee all departments, including in-patient treatments, surgery, and the Neonatal Intensive Care Unit. He has now spearheaded the project of a psychology department. Charlotte's position would be Chief of Pediatric Psychology, overseeing both in- and out-patient services. He went on to say that Charlotte would have two head nurses who would work directly for her and oversee the daily operations. Of course, there would be an extensive care team of specialists trained to treat a wide variety of psychiatric conditions.

"I have already asked Catherine to consider moving over as one of the head nurses," he said with a smile. "Together, you two would work to hire a second head nurse and all of your support staff. I asked Catherine to join us this morning so you two could see if the fit might be right as you consider our offer."

Charlotte replied genuinely, "Oh yes, that is an amazing plan. Catherine seems like the perfect fit and I think we would work together well! Thank you for taking the time to spend with us this morning, and I look forward to coffee tomorrow."

"Of course! And my door is always open!"

Catherine left, and Dr. Richards explained that Catherine was his only decision, assuming she accepted the offer.

"I know and trust her; she has a proven strong work ethic and rapport with all the doctors and nurses here."

He had names and thoughts on options for her staff, but they would get to it when the time was right. Charlotte listened carefully as he talked more about his vision coming to reality. Initially, there would be four in-patient rooms, with room to grow to eight. There would be therapist's offices for out-patient care, two solitary sensory rooms, a family conferencing room for conversations with hospital staff, and a high-tech, family-friendly waiting room. This in-patient unit would also include four overnight suites for families who need it. He also explained that there was room to grow because the out-patient clinic offices and therapy rooms were on the other side of the building.

Charlotte's mind was blown. She could hardly believe any of this. Her mind was already spinning with thoughts and possibilities, so she had to take a moment to slow herself down. Atticus then explained that the two floors at the other end of the building would be for out-patient therapies. He wanted Charlotte to organize and arrange everything as she saw fit, both getting started and leaving room to grow. Atticus had the builders on standby. Not only was it clear that Dr. Richards was proud of this psychology department and its startup plans, but also that he knew that Charlotte would take it further and make it greater, long after his retirement.

Charlotte was honored to be the one Dr. Richards wanted in charge. She felt confident that she could not only do this, but she wanted to do it. She would be happy doing this. *Yes,* she thought. *This is what she wanted.*

"Thank you, Dr. Richards. It was an honor to meet you, and I thoroughly enjoyed our tour today. This hospital is wonderful," Charlotte said both professionally and sincerely.

Back at the B and B, Charlotte couldn't stop smiling. Something felt different inside, and she couldn't help but think it was not only from this interview but also from being back home. The brown horse and her foal came to visit at the fence. They both nickered when Charlotte came closer. She decided to sit in the Adirondack chair and bask in the beauty around her. Charlotte found the horses soothing, and soon, she found herself telling them all about today and coming home.

Paul

Paul wondered if he'd hear from Charlotte after her interview, but he didn't know how long it would last. He decided today he would lay low at home and maybe clean up after a workout. His mind was exhausted from processing all the things that had happened in the last twelve hours. The intense mental energy surrounding the arrest of the Preston brothers and the emotional energy of telling it all to Charlotte had been a lot. It was, however, perfectly balanced out by the comfort and familiarity of having Charlotte over, spending time with her, sharing the hard stuff with her, and having her fall asleep right next to him. He started the coffee maker and changed into gym shorts. The low, looming dark clouds outside threatened a good summer storm, so before it rained, Paul decided to go for a run and then hit the weights. It was a good workout, he thought, and it helped clear his mind.

Paul leaned against the kitchen counter and tried to call Charlotte, but there was no answer. He left a message in her voicemail and decided to go for a shower. The master bathroom was one of his favorite renovations out of all the projects he'd done on the house. He gutted the old, pink, and ivory tiles and replaced them with white marble heated floor tiles, which always felt good on his tired feet. He reached into the doorless shower, shielded only by a wall of glass cubes, turning on the double shower head. Dropping his shorts, he walked into the hot, steamy shower. The view from the shower was one of his favorite features. He had designed the back wall of the bathroom with floor-to-ceiling windows, framing the natural waterfalls and dense trees outside. The lush greenery created a private, almost sensual experience that he cherished. The hot water worked its magic, easing the tension from his shoulders and neck, and he lingered for a few extra minutes, enjoying the soothing embrace.

Wrapping a towel around his waist, Paul stepped out of the shower, the soft fabric brushing against his damp skin. As he walked toward the bedroom, he heard his phone ringing.

"Hey! What are you doing?" Charlotte said with her natural enthusiasm.

"Just got out of the shower," he said nonchalantly. "How did everything go?"

"Paul, it was amazing. You wouldn't believe how awesome the people were, Dr. Richards and this nurse, Catherine. The hospital is gorgeous, and get this: the psychology unit is its own brand-new building in the back of the hospital. It's state of the art, and it will have everything. Dr. Richards has ideas and plans and then I would get to take the reins. I would decide what path the future takes," Charlotte was on overdrive, and Paul wasn't sure if she had even breathed. "I never would've imagined this in my wildest dreams!"

"Well, damn! That's awesome!" He chimed in. "So did he offer you the job yet?"

"No, but I have more meetings tomorrow, and I'm sure he has other candidates to interview. Obviously, he would have other things on his plate, too." She explained. "I can be patient for this. This feels so right!"

"Sweet! Although I've never heard you say you could be patient for anything in your life, so that's a little scary!" he said with a laugh.

"Oh, shut up!" she yelled.

"So, what are you doing now?" he asked her.

"Spending time with the horses. It looks like it's going to rain, but it's so peaceful out here. I feel like I can breathe. I feel like I can think. I feel like I can smile," she said contently.

"Well, you have fun with all your feelings and stuff," he said sarcastically. "Dinner at your dad's is at 5:00. Do you want to ride out there together?"

"I'd love it! I'll be ready at 4:45, don't be late," she said in a sweet, sassy voice.

Atticus

Atticus sat in his office, put his feet up on the desk, crossed his arms across his chest, and smiled. Elizabeth drove from Durham today to be a part of tomorrow's meetings and dinner with Charlotte. Atticus loved that she was there. He told her that she was right, that Charlotte was exactly what this place needed. She was perfect for the job and brings brought more to the table than just her exceptional resume. He picked up his phone and saw he had two missed calls, but he had another phone call to make first.

"Charlotte," he said in his joyful, booming voice, "this is Atticus Richards."

"Dr. Richards, hi! How are you? Thank you so much for all your time today; your facility is absolutely fantastic. I am looking forward to the meeting tomorrow with Catherine. Were you able to line up those others?"

"I was. We can go over the agenda tomorrow morning. But Charlotte," he said, his tone firm yet warm as he leaned forward slightly, trying to stay focused, "I am calling because I'd like to offer you the job. It's all yours if you want it." He paused, a genuine smile playing at the corners of his mouth. "You exceeded all our expectations and then some. You will be an excellent addition to our pediatric family. I wanted to call you as soon as I got the paperwork finished," Charlotte listened intently, her eyes widening with anticipation. "We'd like to offer you a starting salary of $250,000 with full benefits, six weeks' vacation, and a relocation stipend." There was a brief silence on the phone. "Of course, take all the time you need to think it over. And let me know if you have any issues or questions about the offer."

"Oh!" Charlotte exclaimed, her surprise evident. "Dr. Richards, I don't know what to say."

"Say yes," he replied quite softly. "Come be a part of our family."

Charlotte smiled, a mixture of joy and disbelief on her face. "Is it okay if I take a little time to process everything and then call you back?" she asked, her voice tinged with emotion.

"Of course, I know there's a lot to consider with moving your life back here. Give it thought, and just let me know whenever you feel ready. I actually was able to line up the meetings for you tomorrow after your coffee with Catherine if you'll still consider another day here." Someone peeked in the door, and Atticus waved her in while he continued talking. "I have spoken to the builder, the HR staffing manager, and two therapists I'd like you to meet. Elizabeth and I would like to take you to dinner after your long, busy day tomorrow. Whether you have a decision by tomorrow or not does not matter to me at all. We both look forward to seeing you in the morning."

"Thank you, Dr. Richards. I am truly thankful for this opportunity and also for your generous offer. This is the job of a lifetime. I will let you know my answer as soon as I can, and of course, I will absolutely be there tomorrow."

Atticus hung up the phone and looked at Elizabeth sitting on the couch. "If she says yes, everything will be perfect."

"Well." he said, pausing to go sit beside her, "almost perfect."

"Atticus, I have a good feeling about this," she said, smiling.

"I do, too," he looked into her eyes and took her hands in his. "Though I find myself in a tough situation. I'm now waiting on answers from two different women. Elizabeth…," he trailed off before being interrupted.

Her phone rang as she said, "Which answer do you think you'll get first?" giving him a wink. "Hello, this is Dr. Elizabeth Marsh."

Charlotte

Charlotte took a deep breath, "Hi, Dr. Marsh. This is Charlotte Masters. I had the pleasure of interviewing with you last week. I am thankful you found the right fit for your practice, and I appreciate you letting me know," without much of a pause, Charlotte continued in her professional voice. "I am calling to tell you thank you. I just spent the day touring and interviewing with Dr. Richards at Blue Ridge Memorial Hospital. He told me you personally recommended me, and so I owe you a huge thank you."

"Oh Charlotte, there is no thanks needed. I know you needed more than part time. I know you needed more than staying in your comfort zone. You are destined for big things. It was obvious from the second you walked through my door," Elizabeth said with a confident voice. "Dr. Richards has the experience, the resources, and the vision to start you on the path you want. I just couldn't offer that at my practice. You will be able to do all the big things you could ever imagine over there."

"Wow, I have all those same thoughts, too! So, thank you so much, Dr. Marsh. I hope our paths cross again in the future."

"Me too, dear," she said, smiling.

It had just started to sprinkle outside when Charlotte hung up with Dr. Marsh. She had a few hours before Paul was picking her up, so she walked across the lawn and into her clean, cozy room. She couldn't wait to tell everyone at dinner all about her day, but first, she had a very important phone call to make. Then, she decided to snuggle into her heavenly bed and nap.

Chapter 8
2022

Hannah

Driving to pick up Charlotte for their girls' getaway weekend gave Hannah a little time to decompress from the difficult week at school. She usually loved the fast-paced, unexpected life of being a principal, and this one would be one for the books. One teacher went into labor; her water broke in the cafeteria. One teacher had to leave because of a death in the family, and then another one just flat-out quit. *Who does that?* Her chest hurt thinking about it all and how much she needed to do. Her Assistant Principal, Amy, had already made phone calls and had plans in motion. She told Hannah to have a great weekend and not to worry about school. Hannah turned into Charlotte's driveway and honked the horn. Despite their busy schedules, they always made time for an annual girls' getaway weekend. She couldn't wait to hear what Charlotte would have to say about all this.

It was Hannah's turn to choose their destination this year, so they were making the drive to a luxurious spa nestled in the serene countryside just outside of Richmond, VA. For the next hour, they talked about the situations with Hannah's teachers at school, Charlotte's home renovation, and what was going to happen to the diner now that Molly decided to retire. After they vented about their daily lives, both girls could start to feel their tension release. As they pulled the car under the grand portico, their excitement was palpable, eagerly anticipating a weekend of pampering and rejuvenation.

The resort itself was a haven of tranquility, nestled amid rolling hills and lavish gardens that seemed to stretch endlessly into the horizon. The air smelled faintly of jasmine, adding to the serene ambiance. Upon check-in, a frosted glass of bubbly champagne was handed to them, the coolness of it refreshing against their fingers. The girls clinked their glasses, toasting to friendship and the promise of a relaxing getaway, their laughter blending with the soft breeze. They made their way to their suite, where the luxurious atmosphere felt like a world away from their daily lives. Stepping out onto the balcony, they were greeted by a breathtaking view of the sun dipping behind the hills, casting the landscape in warm golden hues. They took their champagne outside, the bubbles dancing on their tongues as they sipped, enjoying the quiet. The girls ordered room service, changed into pajamas, and turned on a movie called *Nobody Will Believe You*. Neither of them had heard of it but settled in for an always-captivating *Lifetime* movie.

"Thanks for planning all this. It's perfect," Charlotte said to Hannah.

"Of course! This was an easy choice!" she replied. "It's heavenly!"

Hannah noticed Charlotte looking at her phone and sending a quick text.

"Everything okay?" She said without pausing, "Can you believe this shit?" Hannah yelled at the movie. "She's just being nice and trying to make friends, but someone hacks into her phone? And now, whoever this is is stalking her! *Lifetime* sure knows how to make drama out of anything!"

"Thank goodness we didn't have all this cell phone drama when we were in high school," Charlotte said, shaking her head with a half-smile, her fingers absentmindedly tracing the rim of her glass.

Hannah's eyes widened in sudden realization. She shot Charlotte a glance, raising her eyebrows as she sucked in a quick, excited breath. Her hands flew up, and she leaned in closer, almost bouncing in her seat. "You know who this sounds like? You know who would've done this shit back in high school?" Hannah said, getting quite animated now.

Charlotte just looked at her.

"Becky! That girl that wanted to date Paul, or did date Paul, or whatever. The girl you couldn't stand!" Hannah continued to be animated, standing up and jumping on the bed. "She was always just showing up everywhere, like she was stalking us, or y'all, or just Paul! Oh my gosh!"

"Oh, yes!" Charlotte jumped up, too. "I hated her! All she wanted to do was have Paul to herself. Remember she never showed up at the summer party? What year was it? Was it 1996? Paul was so bummed because she never showed up? I wonder whatever happened to her?"

"Oh yes! That was the night of my first kiss!" She laughed. "Hell, if I know! I remember Luke and Paul mentioning her name a few times in college, but that was forever ago! Although, you know, she could be stalking us right now!" The girls fell on the bed with laughter. It was the perfect first night away.

After the movie, the girls laughed about how tired they were, and it was only 9:00 pm. They brushed their teeth, turned out the lights, and said good night. Charlotte didn't even look at her phone when she heard a text come through. They both slept better than they had in a long time, actually a year ago, to be more exact.

Charlotte

The next morning, Charlotte and Hannah began their day with luxurious indulgence and customized pampering. They started with a two-hour massage that melted away weeks of stress. Enhanced with the soothing scents of lavender and sage, two hours went by like a midnight dream. Next, they took a dip in the heated mineral pools that promised to detoxify and revitalize their bodies. Hannah joked about how they'd have to stay in the pool all day in order to achieve complete revitalization of her body! Lunch and champagne were served poolside. Between the bites of cucumber sandwiches, sips of refreshing champagne, and laughter-filled conversations, they caught up on more personal situations and even talked about dreams for the future. The day wrapped up with a pedicure, manicure, and facial, each just as heavenly as the other. Walking back to their room, they laughed about feeling somewhere between a walking Jell-O cup and a drunk college girl. Back in their room, they lay down for a while and then changed for dinner.

The ambience of the hotel restaurant was relaxing, with soft music and a warm fireplace crackling in the background. The light from the fireplace danced around, casting warm glows onto tables filled with happy conversations and celebrations. A bottle of chilled Moscato was brought to the table, and the girls toasted to friendship and the future.

Charlotte and Hannah started their meal with a crisp, refreshing salad tossed in a tangy balsamic vinaigrette dressing. Then they dined on perfectly-aged ribeye steaks, seared to medium-rare perfection with a rich, caramelized crust. The juicy meat inside had their tastebuds going wild with its infusion of butter and herbs. The steaks were complemented by crispy golden carrots seared in grape seed oil and creamy garlic mashed potatoes. The girls decided to share a rich chocolate lava cake for dessert. The warm cake and molten center were perfectly combined with hand-churned vanilla ice cream. Over the two and a half hours at the table, Charlotte and Hannah laughed over more stories and memories they must have told each other hundreds of times.

The girls enjoyed sleeping in on Sunday morning before packing up and hitting the road back home. Charlotte and Hannah found themselves feeling rejuvenated and their friendship closer than ever. The spa weekend had not only pampered their bodies but had also nourished their souls.

Paul

With a quiet weekend at home, Paul spent Saturday mowing the lawn, weed eating and trimming hedges. He still loved the hard labor of a long day in the yard. Later that evening, he met a buddy for some beers at Black Ox. Paul was up early Sunday morning, made coffee, and settled in at the dining room table. He had decided to start working on the cold case file he had recently been assigned to at work. He was anxious to get into it, especially because his Sergeant told him it was a case from an arrest he made many years ago as a beat cop.

The case file was fat, held together with multiple clips and rubber bands. Inside were details of an unsolved murder spree. There were police reports, witness statements, and photos and reports from multiple crime scenes. There was also a cardboard banker's box full of notebooks and papers from the suspects. The case turned cold not long after they recovered only three of the four bodies the suspects admitted to murdering. As he began to sift through the case file, Paul could sense the weight of the unanswered questions and the responsibility that came with them.

Paul spent hours combing through the initial evidence. The crime scene photos, although grainy and somewhat faded, showed grim details that spoke volumes about the violence of the crime. Paul meticulously reviewed the autopsy report, noting the precise cause of death and the time of the three murders. One woman was murdered in South Carolina, another in West Virginia, and one in North Carolina. According to the suspects' statements, a fourth body was not far away. Paul studied that part of the statement. *Did he mean not far away from the other body or not far away from here?* He scrutinized the witness statements, which were often contradictory, but none of them mentioned seeing two women with the men. Paul's mind was racing.

He poured himself another cup of coffee and started to read the contents of the notebooks. When a detailed drawing of Bud Masters' farm dropped out from one of the notebooks, Paul felt the wind sucked right out of his chest. He couldn't put the notebooks down, reading several of them multiple times. There was one notebook with plans to burn the Masters' farm down, complete with drawings, Bud's comings and goings for months, and other little notes. Then, there was a notebook for each of the victims. Studying these, Paul found cryptic messages throughout the pages that, when he pieced them together, told the names and burial places of the victims.

Sarah Raines, Assurance, West Virginia.

Alice Long, Asbury, North Carolina.

Madeline Falls, Angelus, South Carolina.

Paul couldn't put down the other notebook. He was determined to put together the message. It was after midnight when he did.

Rebecca Williams, Airpoint, North Carolina.

Rebecca Williams.

"Oh my God," he said out loud. "It's Becky."

Chapter 9
2007

Charlotte

Charlotte took her time getting ready for dinner tonight. She enjoyed a long, hot shower, relaxing in the steam, letting the soapy water run from her shoulders, over her breasts, and down the rest of her body. She washed her hair with the fragrant shampoo and conditioner from Herbal Essence, lathered her body with a pure white Dove body bar, and indulged her skin with the Raspberry Tangerine body lotion Shirley had left out for her. She wrapped herself in the lush Elizabeth Arden's boutique Red Door towels, sat at the beautiful, worn, antique vanity, and took her time putting on makeup. Shimmering apricot eye shadow and matching lip gloss frosted her features. Maybelline's Great Lash mascara lived up to its name and accentuated her deep brown eyes. Pleasantly surprised with what she saw in the mirror, she dried and curled her long, caramel-brown hair. She would leave it down tonight. She chose a sage green sundress with little white daisies and spaghetti straps, paired with brown strappy sandals and silver hoop earrings.

She felt happier and more confident than she could ever remember, and it showed when she stepped out into the sunlight.

It was 4:45 on the dot, and Paul was on time, just like he promised. She smiled at him, shut the door behind her, and ran to the truck.

"You're late," he yelled through the window.

"Ha! Never!" she said, tossing her hair off her shoulders and hopping in the truck. "That's your department!"

"Whatever, I'm never late," he said, laughing in defense. He wasn't sure he had ever said this out loud to her before, but out it came, "You look pretty!" And he meant it.

"Well, thanks! You clean up good, too!" Charlotte noticed a subtle scent, and it made her smile inside. "So, Mr. Stone," she said in a sassy voice, "take me away."

The drive out to the farm was smooth, with the windows cracked just enough for the cool breeze to fill the car. Laughter bounced around the cabin as they teased each other over old inside jokes, their voices getting louder with each quip. Every now and then, Paul would glance at Charlotte, his smile wide, the corners of his eyes crinkling with each laugh. Garth Brooks' songs blasted through the speakers, and they both belted out the lyrics, wildly off-key but not caring at all.

In the middle of the chorus, they both reached for the volume knob at the same time, and their hands brushed—just for a second. It was nothing and everything all at once. A sudden jolt of electricity zipped through Charlotte's stomach, catching her off guard. She quickly pulled her hand back, feeling the warmth linger on her skin. For a brief second, she stole a glance at Paul, wondering if he felt it too or if it was just her heart playing tricks on her.

One thing she did know was that being together in his old Chevy pickup was the most natural thing in the world, and she couldn't think of anywhere else she'd rather be.

Molly

Molly was already at the farm when they arrived. She and Bud had planned to grill out, so Molly got there early to help him prep. She was the first one to greet Charlotte and Paul when they arrived at the house. With a huge, contagious smile, she hugged them both and jokingly asked what had taken them so long. Charlotte and Paul exchanged a look and laughed. Bud and Paul went out back for a beer. Molly and Charlotte went into the kitchen for a glass of wine. For about an hour, the men relaxed in the sun, talking and grilling steaks, while the girls gossiped in the shade and played a game of gin.

Dinner was enjoyed at the wonderfully decorated table on the deck. Charlotte noticed the adorable watermelon decor, and it was the picture of a perfect summer dinner. The tablecloth, the cups, the serving bowls, and everything else made it feel like a summertime family picnic. She knew that Molly enjoyed decorating with colorful themes, so Charlotte made a point of praising it. Bud's famous steaks, corn on the cob, pasta salad, and watermelon were the perfect combination for their meal. Molly sat across the table from Charlotte and next to Paul. Bud settled in next to Molly.

They filled their plates, and Molly didn't waste any time to ask about her day. "Okay, Char, when are you going to tell us how the interview went today?" she said enthusiastically.

Without missing a beat, Charlotte exploded with excitement, "Oh my gosh," she said, "it was amazing! I don't even know where to start!"

"Start at the beginning," Paul chimed in. Charlotte rolled her eyes and kept on talking.

Charlotte went on to tell them everything. She talked nonstop like she was on stage, and the audience was captivated by her monologue. She talked about Dr. Richards and how nice he was. She told them, in precise detail, about the new children's psychology building. She talked about Catherine and other staff members, the short and long-term plans, and all of their hopes for the future. When she finished talking, she took a deep breath and smiled.

"I don't even know what to say! This is so exciting! We are so proud of you, Charlotte," Molly said warmly, reaching for her hand and squeezing it.

"Thank you," Charlotte said. It was at that very moment that Charlotte felt a peace come over her. Looking at the three faces of the people who had always been her biggest supporters, she knew she'd made the right decision.

Bud spoke up and asked, "Did Dr. Richards give you an idea of when you might hear back from him?"

Molly chimed in, "Oh, I'm sure it won't be for a few days, right? Aren't you going back for more interview meetings tomorrow?"

"Yes! Tomorrow, I will start the day by having coffee with Catherine. She has detailed plans for initial development, which we will review together. Then, Dr. Richards set up meetings with two potential therapists to join the team, the builder to continue the process of customizing the entire interior of the expansion, and finally, a meeting with the staffing manager in human resources!" Charlotte was invigorated.

"Sweet," Paul chimed in with a mouth full of corn. "That's awesome."

Bud looked at his daughter proudly and said, "Well, whatever you decide to do, we are proud of you, and we support you."

His words brought tears to her eyes as she smiled at him. "Actually," Charlotte said slowly, "Dr. Richards called me this afternoon."

Everyone sat in silence, full of suspense, their eyes glued on Charlotte.

"Dr. Richards offered me the position of Chief of Pediatric Psychology. Can you believe it?" she squealed. "He wants ME! The job is a dream; the salary is amazing, and it comes with full benefits, along with a moving and housing stipend. How about that?" She looked around, wondering which one of them would say something first.

Paul had a coy smile on his face. Bud smiled bigger than she thought he'd ever seen on his face. Molly screamed and jumped out of her seat, practically knocking Paul over to get to her. She hugged her with the greatest excitement.

"Have you made a decision yet? Or are you going to wait and see how tomorrow goes? There's a lot for you to think about, right?" Bud asked.

"Yes! Have you thought about it?" Molly asked.

"Just spill it!" Paul blurted out.

Charlotte was trying to keep herself from exploding and decided to have a little fun with them. She looked at them and said, "Well… I spent the afternoon thinking about everything possible, including all the aspects of the job, graduation in a few weeks, selling the condo and moving, where I'd live," she continued teasing them, "so there's just so much to think about. Like which floor I want to live on, what color I should paint the walls, and a closet big enough for all my shoes and all my clothes, too. Should I get a dog? Maybe I'll get two dogs, a big one and a small one. And I've always wanted to have a fish, so I think I'll get a big fish tank, the kind with the LED lights. I want to know what you all think, too." Charlotte was out of breath, but she kept going. "I'm thinking about going vegan too, ya know, like a total reset. Are there any grocery stores that would have plant-based foods? Oh, there's just so much to think about!"

Paul looked at her with frustration, "Seriously?"

Charlotte burst out laughing.

"No, I'm not serious! You should've seen your faces!" Charlotte had a good laugh. Then she said, "I did actually call Dr. Richards before I came over here and told him I would love to accept the job!" Charlotte squealed.

Everyone erupted with excitement, and when Molly noticed the look on her son's face, she could tell exactly how he was feeling.

"Oh, Charlotte, this is the best news!" Molly said with enthusiasm.

"Sure is, buttercup," Bud chimed in with a smile.

After lots of hugs and a toast to the future, Molly said, "Why don't y'all hang out and talk while Bud and I clean up."

Paul looked at Charlotte and said, "Want to go for a ride?"

"I'd love to," Charlotte said. She grabbed Paul's hand and ran towards the Gator, "Let's go!" She felt like they were fifteen again.

Paul

Paul couldn't get to the pond fast enough, and Charlotte still had no idea. As she drove down the winding path, the Gator left an orange cloud of dust behind them. Charlotte had a smile on her face and her hair blowing in the wind. The anticipation was filling his body with flutters from his chest and a throbbing sensation in his jeans. He designed every detail of this cottage with thoughts of her and used his own two hands to make it come to life. It was full of all the things she loved about home, including a large reading nook by the window and a year-round fireplace. She loved sliding barn doors, kitchen islands, and screened-in porches. Her dad hoped that building a cottage would bring Charlotte home, and Paul hoped it would also make her want to stay. He noticed her squinting to see a light by the pond. He loved how her nose scrunched up when she was trying to see something far away. It was when she realized the light was not coming from the fire pit but a window instead, Charlotte jammed on the brakes. A little white cottage with a forest green door and matching shutters stood across the pond.

"Oh my God! What in the world?" She asked, turning to look at Paul. "When... How... Did you know my dad built this?"

Dodging her question, Paul hopped off the Gator, saying, "Let's go check it out!"

There beside the pond, against a curtain of luscious American Beech and Sugar Maple trees, the small cottage spilled soft, golden light from its windows. The steeply pitched thatched roof with golden straw gave the cottage an almost fairytale-like appearance. A small wreath made from magnolia leaves hung on the front door. It was just the start of the cottage's rustic charm. The two of them strolled up the dusty path leading to the front steps, their dreamy souls thinking about what lies inside. Paul pulled the key from his pocket and unlocked the door. Before stepping in, Charlotte took special notice of the rocking chair and table on the porch. She thought the woodwork looked homemade.

Inside was warm and inviting, with the scent of aged wood and hearth smoke lingering in the air. Paul chose wide-planked, whiskey barrel oak floors that made you want to take off your shoes and slide into Muk Luks cabin socks. A grand stone fireplace commanded the attention of the room. Above it, a mantelpiece displayed a piece of hand-crafted pottery, antique candle sticks, a few small trinkets, and a picture frame. The oversized, plush sofa and chairs were arranged around a worn, heirloom coffee table made for sinking into comfort. On the other side of the room, a cozy reading nook beckoned with an overstuffed armchair and a small side table piled high with well-worn books and a small reading lamp. The large windows, draped with simple linen curtains, allowed nature's beauty to come inside. Charlotte noticed a gentle breeze stirring leaves in a ballet of whispered secrets.

The heart of the cottage was its quaint kitchen. Polished stone countertops and a farmhouse sink complemented white-washed cabinets with wrought iron handles. A repurposed, vintage secretary desk displayed a collection of ceramic dishes and glassware, including pink drinking glasses embossed with hearts and ivy. They reminded Charlotte of the ones her mother had when she was a child. So did the secretary's desk. It made her pause for a minute. A small, wooden dining table with mismatched chairs sat in the corner, perfect for intimate meals. The kitchen was equipped with modern appliances that blended seamlessly with the rustic decor, including a sleek, stainless steel stove and a retro-style refrigerator.

"Who did all this?" She said to Paul, running a finger along the countertop. Walking over to the large barn door on the other side of the cottage, she said, "Isn't this incredible?"

She was in total awe when she slid the barn door open and gazed into the master bedroom. It was a serene retreat with a large four-post bed adorned with a patchwork quilt and an array of plush pillows. Tucked in the far corner of the room was an old dresser and cozy armchair. A large, braided rug added warmth to the wooden floor, while sheer lace curtains framed the picturesque window overlooking the pond. Hanging on the wall above the bed was a large, framed photo, one that had been taken on her family's farm many years ago. It showcased the old red barn and Charlotte's childhood horse, Magnolia. Staring at the picture inquisitively, it took Charlotte a minute, but then it all hit her at once.

Charlotte

She turned around slowly and saw Paul leaning against the doorway. It was clear now. "Oh my God," she said softly, "You did all this, didn't you?"

Her very best friend, who had been by her side for her entire life, stood there with a new vulnerability. "How? When?" she found herself stumbling over her words.

At that moment, in the new silence, Charlotte realized that her feelings for Paul had evolved into something more profound. Her stomach fluttered with anticipation when she realized what he had done for her. Paul looked at her, the girl he had always loved, but tonight, she was more than just his best friend – she was the woman he couldn't imagine living without. His heart pounded in his chest, a wild mix of fear and longing. It was as if he was seeing her for the first time, yet also realizing she had been the most important part of his life all along. The air between them was charged, heavy with unspoken words and pent-up emotions.

He hesitated for a moment, the weight of what he was about to do pressing down on him. What if this changed everything? What if she didn't feel the same? But the thought of never knowing, of letting this moment slip away, was unbearable.

He wanted to take in every second of this experience together. He went to her and stood closer than he ever dared before. The warmth of her skin under his touch sent a shiver down his spine.

He cradled her face and kissed her with a passion she never knew existed. She matched his intensity. She didn't want him to stop, but he pulled back and looked deeply into her eyes. "Charlotte," he whispered, his voice thick with emotion. "I don't know how to say this without it sounding like it's been said a thousand times before, but I can't keep it in any longer. I love you." He said, the words tumbling out in a rush, raw and unfiltered. It felt like ripping his heart open and laying it bare before her. "I have loved you for as long as I can remember. It's always been you."

"Paul," she whispered, reaching for him, her hands finding the top of his jeans. She looked up at him and said, "I love you, too." The words took his breath away. He lightly pressed his lips to hers. This kiss was gentle, but as it deepened, they finally succumbed to years of unspoken desires and needs.

She felt lips move to her cheek and then to her neck. It was slow. Charlotte closed her eyes and exhaled. A spark ignited, sending an electric wave of warmth and eroticism through them both. Paul took his time, tasting her skin with each kiss. There were no questions, no expectations, and no distractions. He pulled her closer as she slowly slid her hands up his sides, sliding his shirt up his warm skin. He finished taking it off and tossed it on the floor, but he never took his eyes off her.

She ran her hands over his chiseled stomach; his skin was warm. She kissed his chest from one side to the other. His body responded with a strong erection, and she didn't stop. Her body ached for more, and he could feel it. He wanted all of her. Feeling her lips on his skin, Paul's fingers found the straps of her sundress. He slowly slid them off her shoulders, letting her dress fall to the floor. She had nothing on underneath. He looked at her, standing there bathed in the soft glow of candlelight, her figure unveiling the curves of her body, both delicate and strong.

Paul

He buried his face into the nape of her neck. Her skin smelled like raspberries, her hair like wildflowers. His body craved more of her. Paul felt her hands unbuckling his belt with an urgency to have him naked, too. When his pants hit the floor, he lifted her up, her legs around him. He could feel the heat between her legs against his stomach. Paul held her tightly, feeling her against his skin. Within just a few steps, he laid her gently on the bed. They paused to feel the intimacy and intensity of that moment. They just had to look at each other to know what they each wanted.

His lips found her breasts perfectly supple and already hard. Her hands slowly ran through his thick hair and traced paths on his suntanned back. She felt his erection on the inside of her thigh and was exhilarated by its heat and pulsation. Her arousal was heightened as she moved her hips in rhythm with him. She wanted him to be inside her. When she whispered yes, they shared an electric experience neither of them knew could exist. They stayed tangled together, giving each other earth-shattering pleasure. It was a night of unforeseen perfection.

Charlotte

As the first rays of dawn peeked through the window, Charlotte stirred awake. Blinking sleepily, she found herself enveloped in warmth and comfort. There was a promise of new beginnings in the silence. Turning her head slightly, she looked at Paul lying beside her, his face relaxed in sleep, framed by tousled dark hair. His arm was draped gently over her waist, holding her close as if unwilling to let go even in slumber. She couldn't help but smile as she traced the contours of his face with her eyes, taking in the familiar lines that were becoming things she'd remember for the rest of her life. Lying here together in the quiet morning, Charlotte felt a rush of gratitude for this moment. She shifted slightly, causing Paul to stir. His eyes fluttered open, and a sleepy smile spread across his face when he saw her looking at him.

"Hey you," he murmured, his voice husky with sleep.

"Hey," she replied softly, reaching up to brush a lock of hair from his forehead. "Did you sleep well?"

Paul nodded, tightening his hold around her slightly. "How could I not?"

She whispered to him, "I want to stay like this always."

He squeezed her tight and said, "Always." At that moment, it became clear that they had been made to fit together all along.

They rested in bed together after more mind-blowing sex - couldn't get enough of each other. However, they decided on breakfast, and Charlotte noticed that the fridge and pantry were completely stocked.

"Molly?" she asked with a smile.

"Yes," he said, wrapping his arms around her waist. He kissed her neck, just because.

Charlotte made scrambled eggs with bacon and toast, as Paul opened the sliding glass doors to the screened-in porch. A light breeze brought in fresh air. The cottage was filled with the aroma of comfort food. Paul made coffee for two and went out on the porch. Charlotte turned on the radio, filled their plates, and joined him.

"This is absolute heaven. I still can't believe you did all this for me." At that moment, a flock of ducks flew in and landed in the pond. Charlotte felt like she was seeing the pond for the very first time, even though she'd seen it all her life.

"I love you, Charlotte."

"I love you, too."

They spent the better part of the morning reminiscing and teasing each other at this turn of events. They talked about what they wanted their future to look like. They discussed the timing of things when she returned to Durham at the end of the week. She needed to finish her dissertation and had already set the date to defend it. Paul already planned on coming to graduation, so they decided to pack up most of her things that same weekend and bring them back to Eagle Valley. Charlotte beamed with joy at the thought of getting settled into her perfect cottage. It was her perfect cottage built by her perfect man.

A song came on the radio that took them back to a certain summer night. They looked at each other and broke into laughter.

Charlotte sang, "Some'll win, some will lose."

Paul jumped to his feet and belted out, "Some are born to sing the blues!"

And in perfect unison, they finished the stanza, dancing around the screened-in porch. "Whoa, the movie never ends; it goes on and on and on and on."

Their midnight train would take them to an unbelievable future. The movie was theirs to make.

Chapter 10

2022

Charlotte

The morning of the promotion ceremony, Charlotte and Paul had breakfast together before the kids got up. It would be a beautiful summer afternoon, perfect for an outdoor event. Charlotte loved the laziness of Sunday mornings, getting up early before the kids. It was a special time for her and Paul. Today was extra special. She was so proud of him. He loved his job and worked hard for their family. Today, he would become Sergeant Paul Stone.

She knew that Paul felt like all his years with the Roanoke County Police Department had paid off. Becoming a detective seven years ago was a natural transition for him. He loved the detective work. The decision to take the Sergeant's exam was not a light one. Both of their kids were now in elementary school, and Charlotte's career was changing pace. She knew he was worried about the time commitment that came with the Sergeant title, but she sweetly reminded him that their family is a team and their schedules would work themselves out.

Paul had to get to the ceremony earlier than Charlotte and the girls. He was irresistible in his full uniform, actually any part of his uniform. When he kissed his wife, he noticed her hair smelled like wildflowers, and the curves of her body still took his breath away. Charlotte still felt flutters in her stomach when he kissed her, even after all these years. He gave the girls a wink and a fist bump. They smiled and said bye. They loved their dad, and he loved them more than he ever thought possible. Charlotte wondered what she had done to be this happy.

She and the girls pulled into her driveway just as Hannah flew out of her front door and into the front seat of the car. Charlotte loved that her best friend had not changed a bit. Hannah told stories and laughed with the girls for the entire ride together. She was the life of the party. The girls had been calling her Aunt Hannah since the day they could talk, and Hannah said they had good taste in choosing family members.

In addition to her carload of girls, Charlotte's dad, accompanied by Shirley, would be at the ceremony. Paul's mom greeted them in the parking lot with her usual warmth and enthusiasm. The girls ran to their MeeMaw and hugged her tight. Charlotte heard Molly whisper to the girls that she had candy in her purse. It made her smile.

"Big day, sweetie," Molly said, putting her arm around Charlotte.

"It sure is. I'm so proud of him."

"He's proud of you too, ya know. He is the luckiest husband around," she said warmly.

"Thanks, Molly, I love you." She squeezed her back and tried to keep back tears that were already starting to well up.

"Love you more, kiddo." That actually made a tear run down her cheek.

Paul

Paul stood on the make-shift stage of the beautiful lawn at Eagle Valley City Park. A large American flag was the backdrop of the stage, accented by red, white, and blue balloons and flowers. The weather was hot, but there was a gentle breeze. Paul looked out and saw his family and the huge smiles on their face. Paul's new boss, Captain Thomas, gave his introduction speech, and Paul listened to his words with a heart of gratitude. He took a deep breath before he walked to the stadium.

Good afternoon,

Thank you all for being here. I am deeply humbled to stand before you today. This moment is not just a personal milestone but a reflection of the incredible support I've had along the way. Policing is not a job one can do alone, so I would like to take a moment to express my gratitude.

To my family, you have stood by me with support and encouragement throughout this journey, and I am forever grateful for your sacrifices. Your belief in me has given me the confidence to take on new challenges. You have continuously inspired me to become the best version of myself.

To my mentors and colleagues, I have learned so much from each of you. Your guidance and wisdom have shaped my career in so many ways. Thank you for your trust and confidence in my ability to lead and serve.

Lastly, I want to thank the community we serve. Your trust and respect mean everything. Myself and the Roanoke City Police Department continue its commitment to protect and serve you.

In closing, I am honored and humbled to accept the rank of Sergent today in front of you all. I pledge to uphold the values of our department and will strive for excellence in all that I do. Thank you again for being here with us today.

After pleasantries with other officers and their families at the ceremony, Paul told his family he'd love to celebrate with lunch at Molly's. Love surrounded their table, and the company filled their souls. They talked over pulled pork, corn, baked beans, carrots, mashed potatoes, and sweet tea. Paul looked around the table and thought one thing. He thought about how lucky he really was.

Hannah

The morning after the ceremony, Hannah had an interview with a first-time teacher who applied for the Kindergarten teacher vacancy. Her Assistant Principal, Laura, had lined up the interview last week, and Hannah was grateful. They were both excited about the potential of this new teacher. They reviewed the questions they each wanted to ask and walked together to welcome Miss Brooks.

"Good morning, Miss Brooks. Thank you for joining us this morning. I'm Principal Hannah Pruitt, and this is Assistant Principal Laura Jackson," Hannah said warmly. "Thank you for meeting with us today," Hannah began, her tone encouraging.

They all sat at the table in the conference room. "We know this is your first interview as a teacher, and we're excited to learn more about you and your approach to teaching," Laura said.

Her nerves settled slightly. "Thank you so much for having me."

Hannah pushed her oversized reader glasses up on her nose and leaned forward with interest. "Why don't we start with why you decided to become a teacher?"

Miss Brooks took a deep breath and smiled. "I've always loved working with kids. During my time in college, I volunteered at after-school programs and tutoring centers. I was able to help students master foundational skills by meeting their specific needs at their learning level. It made me realize that teaching wasn't just a job, but it's my passion."

Hannah nodded thoughtfully. "That's wonderful." She looked over at Laura for the next question.

"Can you tell us about a specific experience during your student teaching that particularly stood out to you?"

She smiled, her eyes lit up. "Definitely. I had a third-grade student named Lily who struggled with reading comprehension. We had been working on a story, and she was having a hard time connecting the dots. I decided to try a new approach by incorporating oral storytelling and visual aids. After just a few days, she finally grasped the theme of the story. Her face beamed with excitement. It was an incredible feeling to see her so proud of her progress."

Principal Pruitt leaned back, clearly impressed. "It sounds like you have a solid plan. Lastly, do you have any questions for us or anything you'd like to share?"

"Yes, actually. I'm curious about the professional development opportunities. I feel that it's important for teachers to continue learning and growing as a teacher," she asked professionally.

Mrs. Pruitt and Mrs. Jackson smiled warmly. "We offer various workshops and mentorship programs throughout the year. In fact, during every teacher's first year, they are teamed up with a veteran teacher as their mentor. Our administration is truly committed to supporting our teachers 'growth."

Her face brightened. "That sounds fantastic. I'm really excited about the possibility of working here and joining your already amazing school."

Hannah and Laura walked her to the front of the school. "Thank you for taking the time to come and meet with us, Miss Brooks," Hannah said.

"Please, call me Charlie. I appreciate you both having me here."

"Of course, Charlie. I really love that name!" Hannah said with enthusiasm.

"Oh, thank you, it's quite a story, actually!"

"Do tell," Laura said with sincere curiosity.

"Well, I was adopted after my mother died, just after my tenth birthday. She was a single mom, and I had never known my dad. She told me that he didn't even know I existed. But the biggest thing I really remember her telling me over and over again was that she named me after the woman my father actually loved. I've decided to start looking into finding him, and I'm pretty sure both of my birth parents grew up somewhere around this area." She hesitated, embarrassed that she unloaded that information. "I'm sorry, that's such an overshare," she said boldly.

"Not at all, no need to be sorry," Hannah said. "You were right, and this is quite a story! Do you have any information about your father to help you find him?"

Charlie replied with excitement, "I do. I know his name! I am looking for Mr. Paul Stone."

THE END